FRIDAY NIGHT

Stage Lights

Also by Rachele Alpine

Operation Pucker Up

You Throw Like a Girl

Best. Night. Ever.

A Void the Size of the World

FRIDAY NIGHT
Stage Lights

RACHELE ALPINE

Aladdin M!X
New York   London   Toronto   Sydney   New Delhi

This book is a work of fiction. Any references to historical events, real people, or real places are used fictitiously. Other names, characters, places, and events are products of the author's imagination, and any resemblance to actual events or places or persons, living or dead, is entirely coincidental.

ALADDIN M!X
Simon & Schuster Children's Publishing Division
1230 Avenue of the Americas, New York, New York 10020
First Aladdin M!X edition September 2018
Text copyright © 2018 by Rachele Alpine
Cover illustration copyright © 2018 by Melissa Manwill
Also available in an Aladdin hardcover edition.
All rights reserved, including the right of reproduction
in whole or in part in any form.
ALADDIN and related logo are registered
trademarks of Simon & Schuster, Inc.
ALADDIN M!X and related logo are registered
trademarks of Simon & Schuster, Inc.
For information about special discounts for bulk purchases, please
contact Simon & Schuster Special Sales at 1-866-506-1949 or
business@simonandschuster.com.
The Simon & Schuster Speakers Bureau can bring authors to your live event.
For more information or to book an event contact the Simon & Schuster
Speakers Bureau at 1-866-248-3049 or
visit our website at www.simonspeakers.com.
Cover designed by Jessica Handelman
Interior designed by Hilary Zarycky
The text of this book was set in Adobe Garamond Pro.
Manufactured in the United States of America 0818 OFF
2 4 6 8 10 9 7 5 3 1
Library of Congress Cataloging-in-Publication Data 2018947181
ISBN 978-1-5344-0459-5 (hc)
ISBN 978-1-5344-0458-8 (pbk)
ISBN 978-1-5344-0460-1 (eBook)

To the greatest nieces and nephew in the history of the world:

Brooklyn, Addie, Ellie, Calvin, and Maggie

—Love, Aunt Ray Ray

Chapter 1

Most people would say the best way to watch a Leighton High School football game is cheering the team on to yet another victory, in between bites of Frito pie and sips of Dr Pepper.

I would disagree with them.

Because to me, the best way to watch a Leighton High School football game was with the volume on your earbuds turned all the way up so you couldn't hear anything around you.

That's how I watched all of my stepbrother Tanner's games.

Tonight, I had Tchaikovsky playing at full volume. It was easy to get lost in the music and pretend I was back home at my old dance studio. I could almost feel the creaky wood floor in the changing room and see the sunlight as it streamed through the tiny windows in the main practice space. My eyes might have looked as if I were following the players on the field, but really, I was picturing myself back in my favorite place in the world, leaping and moving so fast it would make you dizzy to watch. I'd just imagined myself taking off into a grand jeté when a finger jabbed me in the shoulder.

"Brooklyn, stand up," my friend Mia whispered and gestured toward everyone around us. The whole stadium was on their feet as they clapped like crazy.

Well, everyone except me.

"You could at least cheer," she said and shoved one of her red-and-white pom-poms into my hand.

"I have no idea what's going on," I said but waved the pom-pom in the air and yelled along with everyone so it looked as if I'd been paying attention.

Mia rolled her eyes; she was used to my cluelessness to football, which in a town that lived football was a rare feat. I'm pretty sure the elementary school classes taught the stats of all the players who ever played for Leighton High and you couldn't pass on to the next grade until you could recite all of the big games and their outcomes.

"Go, go, go," Mom shouted.

"Yes, go, go, go!" I repeated, even though I didn't know what was going and where it was going to. But if I had to place a bet, I'd say it had something to do with Tanner. He was the star of the team and most likely in the process of doing something that would make the town love him even more. As if that were possible. I mean, he had a pizza named after him at Reigert's Pizza Zone, for goodness' sake.

"He did it again! Another touchdown! He's unstoppable!" yelled the man behind me, and Mom clapped her hands together.

"That's our boy!" Stephen high-fived Mom, and the spirit buttons with my brother's face on them that Mom had pinned on her jacket clanged together.

Mia stuck her phone in my face and switched to her journalist voice, which pretty much sounded like her regular voice, except she used words like "eyewitness," "scoop," and "the source." I'd never tell her that, though, because she planned to be a world-famous sportscaster when she was older and took reporting very seriously. She always had the camera on her phone running. In fact, that's how I met her at the back-to-school picnic this summer: She stuck her phone in my face and said she had some questions to ask for a special feature about the new members of Leighton Middle School. I was excited to hear I wasn't the only new person until I found out the other people were a bus driver and janitor. I'm used to her camera now, but at first it kind of felt as if I was the star in a reality show.

"So tell me, Brooklyn. What do you think of Tanner scoring his third touchdown of the game?"

"His third?" No wonder Mom was so worked up.

Mia raised her eyebrows at me.

I changed gears to make it look as if I were really into the game.

"Incredible. His skills on the football field rival any college player right now," I told her, which was what my stepdad Stephen always said.

"Sources say there's talk that he may stay in Texas to play."

I shrugged, figuring the vague approach is best, even if the same talk and speculation in our house was anything but. Mom and Stephen were obsessed with Tanner getting recruited to play college football in Texas, and I swear, Tanner's phone couldn't even ring without one of them getting all worked up that it might be a recruiter.

"The viewers would love to hear your take on the game tonight," Mia pressed on like she does with all her interviews to get down to the truth of the matter, which was probably why everyone at school loved her YouTube channel, *Mia Speaks Sports*.

"Oh, it's absolutely riveting," I told her and made good use of my vocabulary words.

"Really? Can you be more specific? What's been your favorite play of the night?" And now I was sure she was messing with me.

"It's all been good. I can't take my eyes off the game."

She grinned and put the camera down. "My job is to

get the real story out of people. It doesn't work when you lie to me."

Mia knew I didn't watch the game, but my secret was safe with her, which is why she's such a great friend. And it's really one of the biggest scoops around. Could you imagine what this football-crazed town would think if Tanner's stepsister admitted to knowing nothing about the game?

Mia turned to Mom, who is always up for an interview if it means she can talk about Tanner's greatness. "What do you think about Tanner's work on the field tonight?"

"He's unstoppable!" Mom gushed as if she were talking about a celebrity.

I turned away from them and watched the field. Tanner was at the end zone doing his signature dance to Journey's "Don't Stop Believing." He twisted right and left and then twirled in a circle with his arms in the air. The little kids along the fence did it with him. People sang along as the song blasted from the speakers and the cheerleaders faced the crowd and did their traditional push-ups: one for each point Leighton High had on the scoreboard.

"You don't think this is a bit over-the-top?" I asked Mia, who simply laughed, threw her arm around my shoulder, and joined in to belt out the song with everyone else.

It was unbelievable.

This was a high school football game.

High school.

But you'd think that the biggest NFL star in the world had walked across the field.

And I happened to live in that star's house.

It was as if the moment you stepped into this town, the sport infected you. Everyone ate, slept, and breathed football, and if they didn't show up at the stadium on Friday nights, there was no doubt they were listening to it on Sports Radio.

Well, everyone except for me.

Because I only had room for the one love in my life.

Ballet.

I've been dancing since I learned to walk and fully intended to get a spot in the Texas School of the Arts freshman class. The idea of it began the familiar tingle of excitement about what my life could be like. Not only would I get to go to a school that focused on dance all day long, but the teachers there were some of the best in the state. The school graduated amazing dancers who went on to do incredible things. Going to TSOTA would get me one step closer to my ultimate dream of getting into Juilliard's Summer Dance Intensive and one day dancing in a professional company.

The crowd exploded into another round of cheers, and

instead of bleachers full of football fans, I pretended it was from the audience in a packed theater giving me a standing ovation. I turned my music back up and dreamed about a world where it wasn't Friday-night lights that shined down on me, but the bright lights of the stage.

Chapter 2

My alarm blasted way too loud from across the room early the next morning.

"Quiet," I mumbled and tried to burrow back under my sheets. But the alarm wasn't stopping, and I didn't want to wake up the rest of the house, so I crawled back out of the cozy warmth of my bed.

It was still dark outside, so it took me a few seconds to stumble toward it and turn it off. Mom thought I was nuts to get up so early—she always said that sleep was *her* one true love—but there was no way I was going to let the sun wake up before me. The early bird gets the worm, as they say, and I was ready to get all the worms.

Besides, I had a date with someone special.

I crept downstairs into the basement, which was my favorite place in the house because I had my own ministudio.

It sounds crazy, but it's true. It was a surprise that I found out about when we moved here. Mom and Stephen had converted a corner of the basement with a sprung dance floor, giant mirrors, and a ballet barre. I couldn't believe it the first time they took me to see it. I may have broken down in tears, but can you blame me? When dancing is your life, there is nothing more incredible than having your very own studio.

Not to mention that it was such a nice thing for them to do, even if it was near Tanner's stinky weight-lifting stuff. I went down every single morning to work on my stretches and positioning. Dancing there was like a giant hug; it was a place where I belonged, and I loved Mom for it. So while moving here was the worst ever and I missed my old life like crazy, this was a tiny silver lining that could make even the most homesick of days seem better.

I set up my iPad on the tiny table I had against the mirrors and sat on the floor. I was in the middle of a spine stretch when my iPad rang. I pressed the screen and my best friend from home, Dasha's, face filled the screen.

"Brookie! I've missed you," she exclaimed and placed her hand against the screen. I did the same—a virtual high five. Dasha was the only person I'd ever allow to call me Brookie, and coming from her, it was like a little piece of home.

I laughed. "It's only been a week since we last Face-Timed," I told her.

"That's another week I've somehow survived without you," she said, and I couldn't agree more. The two of us had been friends since we were three and our parents enrolled us in our first dance classes together. It was love at first sight for each of us, and we both intended to get a spot in the Juilliard Summer Dance Intensive once we were in high school. We had planned it all out: the days spent studying under some of the best teachers in the world, nights going to the free outdoor performances at Lincoln Center, and weekends spent searching for the best pizza in New York City.

So my first thought when Mom told me we were going to move was, *What am I going to do without Dasha?* It wasn't easy, but we made it work. The two of us might be thousands of miles away from each other, but we weren't going to let anything stop us. Nope. Not a chance.

That was why every Saturday we got up early and taught each other any new steps, positions, and choreography that we'd learned from our teachers. It was like taking a private class with each other and, if you thought about it, pretty brilliant. Besides, FaceTiming with Dasha took a tiny bit of the sting away from missing her so bad. I might not be able to see her in person, but at least I could still dance with her and the two of us could get some girl talk in.

"How is your ankle doing?" she asked, which was the same thing she always asked when we talked.

"It's okay," I said, which was the same thing I always replied back. Short and sweet. I hated talking about my ankle, because for so long it was the only thing anyone talked about. And it had been sore for the last few days, which always made me nervous.

"What about your stepbrother and stepdad? How are things going with your new family?" she asked, checking in on everything that was now so different in my life. That was part of what I loved about talking with Dasha: I could tell her about life in Texas and not have to worry about Mom reminding me to give everything a chance. She'd talked me through my first day of school and listened to me share my fears about joining a new studio.

"They're pretty much the same," I told her. "Which means football, football, football."

"How can so many people be obsessed with one thing so deeply?"

"I know, right? It's not like we're obsessed with one thing."

"No, not at all," she agreed, and the two of us laughed, our mutual passion for ballet stronger than most anything out there.

"So, what's new with you?" I asked. "What did you work on this week in class?"

"Oh my gosh, wait until you see it. I've been dying to talk to you because yesterday Miss Gretchen showed us some of the choreography for our autumn recital, and it's incredible." She backed away from the camera so I could see her entire body and launched into a series of leaps and turns that made me wish even more that I was back home learning this with her. My favorite teacher from Oregon, Miss Gretchen, dreamed up the most amazing choreography, and it stunk that I wouldn't be able to dance any of it live onstage. She was the one who got Dasha and me obsessed with the Juilliard intensive in the first place. She attended when she was in high school and thought we'd be the perfect candidates for it, and I couldn't agree more.

Dasha didn't have a studio space like I did, but she didn't let that stop her. Instead, she danced in her garage. Her parents had put in a space heater and parked outside. They understood how serious she was about her training and wanted to provide a space where she could work. We discovered that if she put her iPad on the shelf above her dad's tool bench, it showed the entire room, which made it easy for us to go over choreography together.

"That's beautiful," I told her when she stopped dancing. I imagined my friends' excitement in my old class when Miss Gretchen had introduced it to them. The days when we first saw a new routine were like presents—unwrapping them to discover the magic inside.

"Miss Gretchen outdid herself," Dasha agreed. "Now let's make sure you learn it too."

And that's what a good friend is for. The two of us

marked the steps over and over again until I was able to dance it as well as Dasha could. We moved together, connected through our screens, and even if we were hundreds of miles away, it was as if we were dancing side by side.

After practicing the song a few times, the two of us paused to catch our breath, and Dasha grinned at me through the screen.

"We're pretty awesome, aren't we?"

"Completely," I agreed. "Juilliard isn't going to know what hit them when they see our audition tapes."

"Forget the intensive; they'll probably offer us full scholarships to the school," she joked.

"And name a building after us," I added. We laughed together so hard that my stomach hurt.

"Okay, you know the drill," Dasha said, growing serious. "Before we say good-bye, it's solo time. Let's see it!" She clapped her hands together as if she were Miss Gretchen getting our dance class's attention.

"Do we have to?" I moaned. "I really don't think I need the practice. I could dance it in my sleep. In fact, I'm pretty sure I do."

"Don't even bother trying to get out of it. You know I'm going to make you run through it," Dasha said and placed her hands on her hips. Even though I was talking to her through a screen, I could feel her stare burning into me, making it clear that she was not going to put up with my excuses.

"All right," I said with about as much conviction as someone headed into a tank full of sharks.

"Come on, show me what you've got. I can't remember what it looks like," Dasha said, which got a smile from me, because the solo I'd been practicing was the exact same one I've danced for over a year. The one I'd performed at my awful, horrible recital. The one I would like to bury somewhere far, far away and never think about it again.

But instead, I danced it every week for Dasha to keep it fresh in my mind. And it would be the dance that I would use as my solo for the All-City Showcase.

Instead of running from your fear, you race headfirst into it.

Isn't that the way it was supposed to be?

But that was easier said than done. Dasha was the only one who had seen my solo since that awful night, and if I had my way, she'd stay the only one. After everything that happened the last time I performed it, the idea of dancing alone in front of an audience again terrified me. And I was doing a good job not having to do just that. I'd promised Mary Rose that I had everything under control, and she said she trusted me, but the problem was that I wasn't sure I trusted myself.

Chapter 3

After I ran through my solo twice, Dasha and I said good-bye and I spread out on the floor to catch my breath. My ankle ached slightly, and I made a mental note to ice it. I was covered in sweat, and my muscles felt as if they were made out of rubber, but that's what I lived for. It meant I had an extra good workout.

I headed upstairs to get something to eat. Mom always made a huge breakfast on Saturday morning for everyone, including a veggie-packed omelet for me to recharge after dancing.

Except today, when I got to the kitchen, the only person there was Stephen. He sat at the table and read the paper with a steaming cup of coffee.

We'd been here for a few months now, but it was still hard to get used to this bigger family. After eleven years of only Mom and me, it was odd to have the size of our family suddenly double. I wasn't used to walking into a room and finding Stephen or Tanner there. And it was all kind of awkward. Mom might have fallen in love with Stephen, but I didn't know him or Tanner the way she did. It's almost as if someone forced you to be friends with someone. Someone who lived in your house, so even if you wanted to avoid them, it was impossible.

And don't get me wrong, it wasn't that I didn't like Stephen. If I had to pick someone to be my stepdad, I'd most certainly pick him. He was always in a good mood, thought up funny lyrics to songs he sang out loud, and made Mom laugh. She seemed so happy when he was around, so Stephen got my vote. But I definitely would've liked him a lot better if he lived in Oregon, and we hadn't had to move our entire lives here.

"Morning, Brooklyn," he said, and gave me a welcoming smile that made it hard for me to hold anything against him.

I gestured at the table.

"No breakfast?" I asked.

"You know the drill. Tanner is still sleeping, so your mom decided to take a shower before he gets up. He had a rough game last night, so it's best to let him rest."

Right. Tanner. How could we even consider eating before he's awake? I swear he gets the royal treatment. The world acted as if he were a king, simply because he could throw a ball down the field. I didn't get it. Not one bit and especially not when I was starving.

My stomach rumbled in protest, and I decided to take matters into my own hands.

"How about I get breakfast started for all of you?" I asked and without waiting for a response, went to the cupboard and pulled out a whole bunch of pots and pans, making sure to create as much noise as possible. Tanner may not be up yet, but I could help with that.

I grabbed the carton of eggs from the fridge, some spinach, a tomato, and mushrooms. I pulled out a bottle of hot sauce that ran empty far too often. I've always been a hot sauce fan, but one of the things I learned that Texas was able to do better than Oregon was make hot sauce. It was incredible, and I pretty much drenched all my food in it.

I'd just cracked some eggs into a bowl when Mom wandered in, her long brown hair making the shoulders of her T-shirt wet. Mom called me her mini-me; everyone said we looked like twins. We both had the same brown eyes, freckles, and noses that turned up a tiny bit at the end. Tanner and Stephen had blond hair and deep tans from the Texas sun. Mom and I, on the other hand, had to lather on the sunscreen wherever we went, because it seemed as if our pale skin burned as soon as we stepped outside.

"Sounds like we're cooking up something very noisy in here," she said as she poured a cup of coffee.

"Veggie omelets," I told her and put the frying pan on the burner a little too hard, so that the spice jars lined up on top of the stove clattered together.

"How about we try to keep it down a bit," Mom said. "Tanner is still sleeping. He needs to rest after all that work last night."

"Heaven forbid we disturb King Tanner. But desperate times call for desperate measures; I'm starving," I said and draped my hand across my forehead and acted as if I were about to faint. "I might perish before he wakes."

"Pretty sure you'll survive," Mom said and ruffled my hair, which thankfully wasn't pulled back into a bun yet, or I would've been mad that she'd messed it up.

"Who's making all this noise down here?" Tanner stood in the doorway in an LHS T-shirt and sweatpants. He had on his glasses, which he hardly wore, and his blond hair was messed up from sleep.

Mom shot me an *I told you so* look.

"Sorry, honey, Brooklyn was a little bit too loud making breakfast," Mom said.

"Some of us have already been up and working out for hours and need to eat before we pass out from hunger," I shot back.

"Give me a break. I had a game last night."

"So I've heard." I shrugged. "I'm just saying, if you want to be the best—"

"Okay, that's enough you two," Mom interrupted.

"You're both amazing athletes. We don't need a competition to see who is the best."

I am, I mouthed to Tanner when Mom wasn't looking. He shook his head and mouthed, *Not a chance*. And as strange as it was to have this new family, it was fun to experience having a sibling—the silly fights and all.

Mom placed a giant glass of orange juice in front of Tanner, and he gulped it down in about five seconds. Stephen brought up last night's game, reliving every moment, play by play. Our weekly Saturday breakfasts were supposed to be about family bonding, but I had a sneaking suspicion it was really just another excuse to talk and talk and talk about football. Basically, it was one big continuation of the night before.

Mom and I had only been in Texas long enough for me to realize that football was almost some bizarre zombielike invasion that got into your brain. Take Mom, for example. We were living a perfectly normal life in Connors, Oregon, and then *BAM!* She met Stephen when he was in town training employees at Mom's company. They dated long distance for a year, got married in a quick ceremony at city hall, and decided it would be best if Mom and I moved to Texas because Tanner was that good at football. They didn't want to take him away from his team, even if it meant I had to leave my dance studio and teachers.

Before we moved, Mom had no idea how the game was played, and now her entire wardrobe is pretty much red-and-white LHS clothing, she hasn't missed one of Tanner's games, and she has hosted the team dinner twice. The fact that she became a football mom didn't even make sense, because the only thing she ever cared about that had to do with football before moving here was who was performing during the Super Bowl halftime show.

As I continued to think about all the ways life was so different now, the room filled with the smells of the breakfast Mom was making for the three of them. I might have taken the healthy route with an omelet, but no one else was following in my footsteps.

Mom set a giant plate of bacon on the table, and Tanner grabbed at least five pieces. He then helped himself to a large serving of the scrambled eggs Mom had prepared. I was sure this wouldn't be his only helping either. Tanner was notorious for going back for seconds and usually thirds. He ate as if he were a bear storing up for a winter's hibernation.

"So what is Coach Trentanelli saying about the defense last night?" Mom asked and sounded as if she'd been talking football her whole life.

"Um, hello, we were all at the game. Remember? Do we have to talk about every single minute of it again?"

I asked, but they ignored me and kept going over every single little detail.

Mom sat down and eased right into the conversation, so I pulled up YouTube on my phone. Mia had posted a new video on her channel. She already had forty-six views and a bunch of comments. I stuck my earbuds in and put my phone in my lap to watch it, although I probably didn't need to—it wasn't like anyone was going to pay attention to what I was doing when there was football to discuss.

"Good morning, Knights country!" she said. "It's great to wake up to a win, isn't it? Oh wait, we've done that every Saturday this season because our team is unstoppable!"

Mia was adorable. She wore her straight black hair in a shoulder-length bob, and her bright blue glasses made her stylish and edgy. Her mom was from Japan, and her dad was from right here in Leighton, and she always said that she was the perfect mix of the two greatest places in the world.

She launched into some commentary that would rival Tanner and Stephen's discussion, and if she had been at our kitchen table right now, she totally could have joined right into the conversation. Mia knew football, and somehow she always managed to get information or a scoop that no one else had. That was why her videos were so popular. Well, that and her on-the-street interviews, where she'd ask anyone and everyone the same question. She would pick one for each video, and it was fun to see all the different responses; they were always a mix of serious, funny, and off-the-wall answers. She was definitely going to be an awesome sportscaster someday.

"Rumor has it that the next generation of Knights may need a few more years before they can fill our LHS boys' shoes," Mia started. "So I went into the crowd at last night's game and asked them myself."

The next shot was of her turquoise sneakers walking up the bleacher steps. She stopped in front of a man with a big bag of popcorn in his hands.

"What do you think of the middle school team's record this year?" she asked.

The man shook his head. "It's looking like they may have a perfect record. A perfect record of no wins." He laughed, but it was true. They'd lost their first three games so far, and I was pretty sure he wouldn't be laughing once the team got to high school.

She interviewed a bunch of people of all ages. Usually, she'd get different responses, but this time they all seemed the same. Everyone agreed; the middle school boys stunk.

I held my phone up and pointed to the video. "Mia said the middle school football team isn't any good this year."

Mom, Tanner, and Stephen stopped talking and

focused on me. Leave it to the mention of football to finally get some attention.

"Aww, did Mia make another one of those fun videos?" Mom asked.

"They aren't fun. She gets a few hundred hits on each of them. And on her new one she interviewed a bunch of people about the middle school team and it doesn't sound as if they're doing too good."

"They're not," Tanner spoke up. "Coach Trentanelli is nervous that they won't be ready for next year."

"They seem as obsessed with the sport as everyone else," I said, but I remembered one of the boys on the team had recently come to school on crutches.

"They're not taking the game seriously enough, and there have been a lot of injuries. They're making mistakes because of it."

"Do they have a personal trainer who can work with them? Maybe someone from the high school?" Stephen asked.

Tanner shook his head. "They've tried that. The boys all think they're awesome and know what they're doing. They aren't willing to listen."

"Yep, that sounds like the boys in my grade," I said and thought about how obnoxious they could be in class, especially on game days, when they acted as if they didn't have to do any work because they needed to focus on preparing for the game.

"Coach is dead set on taking the Dallas Cowboys route."

"The Cowboys route?" Mom asked.

"It sounds nuts, but a few years ago, they added ballet barres outside the locker room to help the team with stretching, and they haven't had as many injuries since. They are going to make the middle schoolers take conditioning classes at some dance studio to help so they can become quicker on the field."

"I bet some parents weren't too thrilled with the idea of their sons taking dance classes," Stephen said.

"Would you be?" Tanner said and laughed. "But what else can they do? They don't want their kids to get hurt and they want them to be better players. You know how it is, Dad. If it helps you win, parents will do it. Remember when Coach had us learning yoga a couple of years ago? He's all about trying random stuff if it means possible wins."

"The team is taking dance classes?" I interrupted, now very interested in the conversation.

"Not dance. Conditioning. Stretching and stuff," Tanner said, and I wanted to be like, *Hello, "stretching and stuff" is a major part of dance.* "He's got some ballet teacher helping out."

"Where?" I asked as a nervous flutter began in my chest.

"I don't know, some studio right by the middle school. Maybe your studio," Tanner said as if it were no big deal.

"You're kidding, right?" I asked and hoped this was a big prank they were pulling on me for some reason, because my studio, Center Stage, was the *only* dance studio near the school.

"Coach needed to do something. Those boys are messing up on the field and will be playing high school ball soon enough. He needs to figure this out before then," Tanner said.

"I think that sounds great, Brooklyn!" Mom said with way too much enthusiasm. "You're always talking about how you wish there were more male dancers. Now you'll have a whole team full!"

"*Dancers,*" I emphasized to Mom, the panic slowly rising in my chest at the realization that this might actually be a real thing. "Not football players. I wanted more boys who were actually *interested* in ballet. This is the worst news ever."

And it was. It really was because ballet was the one place I belonged in this football-obsessed town. The studio was my space and now, just like everything else in my life, football was taking that over too.

Chapter 4

I stormed out of the kitchen and slammed the door to my bedroom.

This was not cool.

Not cool at all.

There was no way those boys were invading my dance studio.

"Over my dead body!" I yelled as I kicked my laundry basket out of frustration. I stubbed the side of my toe and yelped in pain.

I threw myself on my bed and screamed into my pillow.

I was being dramatic and immature, but I had a right to, didn't I? Ever since we moved, nothing was familiar to me. Sure, I had Mia and the girls at my new dance studio, but it wasn't the same. Living in Texas was like being in a country where I didn't understand the language. There were all these customs and traditions that everyone seemed to understand but me. The food was different, the weather was nothing like Oregon, and I missed Dasha and everyone else from my old studio so bad. Ballet was the only thing that made sense, so if what Tanner said about the football players was true, I didn't know what I was going to do.

But what made me even more frustrated was that Mom hadn't even understood how wrong this all was. Instead, she'd told me I should be happy to have the boys at the studio.

Happy.

As if those boys were anything close to serious dancers. The only thing they were serious about was football.

I wanted to text Dasha and tell her what was going on, she'd understand, but she was probably headed to class right now. On Saturdays, we would take a jazz class for fun, as a way to let loose. I wished like crazy I could be there with all of my friends. The class was full of laughing, dancing, and having a great time. The girls at my new studio were supernice, but it wasn't the same. They weren't as serious about dance as I was. Most of them were happy to simply take classes and get a spot on Leighton High School's drill team. They didn't see themselves joining a ballet academy or dancing professionally like a lot of my friends did at my studio in Oregon. Here, dancing was fun, but that was all it was, and I missed that dedication and competitive drive Dasha and my old friends had.

Before I let myself get too upset about what I was missing out on, I grabbed my laptop and lay on my bed.

There was only one thing that could make me feel better.

Thinking about the future.

I went to TSOTA's web page.

The main page loaded, and the pictures I'd become so familiar with popped up; all the images were etched in my mind after spending so long studying them.

A calm came over me as I got lost in the world of the school. I forgot about Tanner and football and the fact that the football team might be invading my studio. Instead, I studied the photos on the website.

It seemed crazy to think that only a few months ago I'd known nothing about TSOTA, especially since it was pretty much all I thought about now. The plan had always been to go to Juilliard's Summer Dance Intensive and hopefully dance professionally one day, but the idea of focusing on ballet while I was in high school was nothing short of amazing. It wasn't until my new teacher, Mary Rose, pulled me aside and told me that she thought I had a good chance of getting in if I was interested that I even learned a school existed that focused entirely on the arts. Of course, you still had to take the usual boring classes like math, English, history, and science, but that was only half of the day. The other half was dedicated to your focused area of study.

Is there anything more wonderful than that?

It was as if the school was made for me. A place where I was surrounded by what I loved. And somehow, someway, I'd convinced Mom to let me audition for the school. When things seemed super lonely here or all mixed up, TSOTA was what kept me going, and I vowed to get one of the spots for incoming freshmen.

I clicked to the page that showed the campus. The outside was nothing special. It was a giant, boring concrete building. The inside looked like any other school, but when you scrolled down farther on the page, it was the other stuff that made my heart swoon. They had a room for dance that took up a huge section of the third floor and was lined with windows. They had eight smaller practice rooms, a yoga studio, and a studio with video gear set up so you could record your dances and watch them back. They had areas for art, music rooms, and a giant theater for weekly public performances. The back of the school was an outdoor garden full of sculptures and benches and a large, grassy area where you could sit in the open air.

I thought about Leighton Middle School and the hallways filled with posters for the football team, the stadium, and the weight room that only those on the team were allowed to use. It didn't take a rocket scientist to understand what my middle school valued, and the idea of going somewhere that praised the arts instead of football filled me with such excitement that it sometimes made it hard to fall asleep at night when I imagined the possibility of being a student there.

I searched the navigation bar at the top of the website and found the link to the page titled "Student Creations." It was my favorite part of the website. The school updated it weekly, and it was full of artwork, photography, and videos of dance and musical performances. I'd examined the technique and skill of all the students in the dance program. I'd compared my dancing to what they could do. And I'd studied their faces and imagined myself dancing alongside of them. It sounded silly, but I'd pretend I went to school here. I could easily imagine the weight of my book bag and dance bag on my shoulders, a familiar melody from a routine I was working on buzzing around in my head, and the way my muscles would ache from dancing every day, but also how alive that would make me. I pictured myself headed to a class or maybe to meet some friends in the cafeteria to swap tips on how to break in our toe shoes or keep our hair in tight, sleek buns. I closed my eyes and could almost hear the music that might come from a practice room down a hallway or the claps of someone who helped keep count as a dancer moved across the floor. I imagined the chemical smell of spray paint and the giant sculpture made out of some kind of shiny material that sat in the back garden.

I thought about everything I had lost when we moved here and everything I might gain if I got into TSOTA.

"Everything you'd gain if you can dance your solo," I said to myself.

"I have to get into that school," I said out loud.

I got up from the bed, stood in front of my mirror, and did a relevé.

"I *will* get into that school," I told my reflection, even if the thought of dancing a solo terrified me.

Chapter 5

I lived in ignorant bliss for the next few days and pretended what Tanner had said about the middle school team was only a rumor. I didn't mention it to any of my friends who went to the studio, because it was best to simply push it out of my mind.

There was this teeny tiny bit of hope that still existed in me that what Tanner was talking about wasn't true. Maybe the classes would be at the school and the boys wouldn't step foot into the studio. Maybe the team was going to a different dance studio. Maybe it wasn't happening at all. Maybe, maybe, maybe. But if there was one thing that I'd learned, it was that wishing didn't always do much good. If it did, I'd be still living in Oregon and dancing with my friends.

Mom pulled into our driveway shortly before dance class was supposed to start. I ran outside with my bag and jumped into the car.

"Sorry I'm running a little late," she told me. "I was on the phone with one of the other players' moms, and I couldn't get her to stop talking."

"It's okay," I told her. "It's not like I'm looking forward to class today."

Mom placed her hand on top of mine and gave me a reassuring pat that didn't help one bit. "Just keep an open mind, honey. Maybe it's not true, and if it is, you never know what they might add to the studio. Maybe you'll be glad that they're there."

"I doubt it," I told her, and it hurt a little that she didn't see what a big deal it was to me. If there was anyone in this world who knew how important dance was to me, it was Mom. She was my biggest cheerleader and always there for me.

Well, almost always, I thought to myself as memories from my horrible, awful recital crept into my mind. I leaned back against the headrest and closed my eyes. *Think about something positive*, I chanted. *Think about something positive.* So I thought about our trip to Portland that we took two years ago and wished more than anything we were back there now.

Shortly after Mom had begun to date Stephen, she'd planned a girls' weekend for us to see *The Nutcracker* in Portland. I'd performed in the show before, but it would be my first time seeing a professional tour, and I could hardly contain my excitement. I watched video after video of the show being performed on YouTube, the girls at my studio got sick of me talking so much about it, and I made a giant countdown chart that I hung in the kitchen, so Mom and I could check off each day as we got closer and closer to the trip.

I couldn't wait to not only see the show but to be alone with Mom since so much of her time had been taken over by Stephen. And we'd get to be together all weekend; since we lived a couple of hours away, Mom had booked a hotel for the trip.

The two of us talked and joked the entire drive to Portland and painted our nails in the fancy bathrobes that were in the hotel room and stayed up late watching movies. I could hardly sleep, and could you blame me? I was about to see *The Nutcracker* the next day!

I'd chosen what I thought was the perfect outfit: a lace dress with long sleeves and a skirt that billowed out around me, white tights, and ballet flats. I had braided my hair around my head like a crown, and Mom had told me I looked like I belonged on the stage.

We went to a fancy restaurant for brunch before the show, but it was nearly impossible to eat anything because all I could think about was how today was the day I got to see a real live professional ballet company. I remember sitting in the seats at the theater almost wishing the show wouldn't start. It sounds weird, but the weekend had been amazing and I was so excited for the ballet that I didn't want it to end. After I watched the show, we would have to leave, and it was back to a life where I had to share Mom with Stephen.

Once it started, though, I was swept away by everything. I was familiar with the dances, sets, and costumes from being in the show myself, but nothing compared to what it was like to sit in the audience and watch a professional company.

It was beautiful, and I couldn't take my eyes off of it.

Mom couldn't either. The two of us were captivated. At one point, when Clara was dancing with the nutcracker toy she had received, Mom turned to me.

"You dance like that," she had whispered, and I got chills. There was no way I danced that well, but there in that theater with the lights down and the music filling my ears, I believed that I could move across the stage like that. I could create magic too. And that was when I promised myself one day that would be me. I would do whatever it took to become a principal dancer.

That weekend had been the best of my life. And not only because I'd gotten to see *The Nutcracker* by a professional company, but because I'd gotten to see it with Mom. And there was nothing better than time where it was just the two of us, especially since as soon as we got home, Stephen was back in the equation again.

I thought about that day the entire drive to the studio. When Mom got there, she stopped the car and reached over to hug me.

"Whatever you find out, you'll be incredible, honey. You're an amazing dancer. It'll all be okay."

"I hope so," I told her and got out of the car, holding her words deep inside of me for courage.

Chapter 6

Most of the class was already in the studio warming up, but before I joined them, I took a minute to catch my breath and prepare myself for what was coming.

I slipped into the changing room and leaned against the wall. The changing room had its usual mess of clothes, bags, and hairpins. The sticky residue of hair spray clouded the mirrors, and after-school snacks and phones littered the top of the long counter that stretched across the length of the room. I breathed in the scents of rosin, perfume, and sweat.

"This place is more of a home than Stephen's house," I said out loud.

It wasn't like Mom and Stephen hadn't tried to make me feel like I belonged. They did. The two of them created that awesome studio in the basement, and Stephen repainted my room the same color it was at my house in Oregon. He even set all the furniture up in the same way. It did look like we transported my room, but everything was a tiny bit off. For example, when I went to sleep at night, I expected to turn over in bed and look out the window, but in the new house there was a door there instead and the window was on the other side of the room, with a streetlamp that made shadows on the walls. Stephen and Tanner liked to keep the air-conditioning cranked up, so you had to pile blankets up on your bed even when it was warm outside, and let's not talk about the time I got up in the middle of the night and ran into Tanner in his boxers. No, seriously, I don't want to talk about it. Ever again.

So my new home didn't seem like, well, home. And that made things a million time worse when you were missing your friends and just wanted something familiar.

But at Center Stage Dance Studio, life was right again. Because when you dance, it's the same everywhere. Arabesque, grand jeté, and relevé don't change. Swanhilda and Franz always get married at the end of *Coppélia*, and the balcony pas de deux in *Romeo and Juliet* will always be one of the most beautiful dances in the world. I have a sticker on one of my notebooks that says DANCE IS THE UNIVERSAL LANGUAGE, which is so true. You could go anywhere in the world, and it would all be the same.

That was why I loved being at the studio. I showed up the first day, Mary Rose had us do a fouetté sequence, and I didn't even have to hesitate, because I knew exactly what she wanted. Unlike Stephen and Tanner's house, where I still have to search for things in the kitchen and forget that it takes the shower forever to heat up, and I jump in when it's still freezing. There was nothing familiar about their house, and sometimes I worried that it would always be that way.

I changed and joined the class on the floor as Mary Rose fiddled with the sound system. I watched everyone for signs that she had mentioned the football team, but nothing seemed different. Elliana's nails were painted her signature bright colors in neon green and blue, Maggie kneeled to stretch her quads, and Adeline licked her hand and tried to tame the million flyaway curls that always escaped her bun, no matter how many bobby pins she used. Everything seemed normal. It was another day in class, which could mean that Tanner had been wrong.

"All right, let's get started," Mary Rose said, and we easily fell into the routine and drills of a typical class. I pushed and moved my body until I was lost in the music and transported to another world where dance was king and football didn't exist.

Jayden grabbed my hand and pulled me into a spin. "You weren't here stretching with us. I thought you'd decided to ditch me."

"Are you kidding? You're never going to be able to shake me," I told him and broke away to do a pirouette.

"Partners for life," he said, and the two of us did the special handshake we'd made up when we promised to try out for TSOTA together.

"How did I get so lucky?" I asked as he spun me around.

And I meant it. Because if it weren't for Jayden, I'd never even try out for the school. I wouldn't have had the courage.

The way it worked here was that there was an All-City Showcase every year that all the dance schools within about an hour radius participated in. You were able to prepare two dances; one solo and one pas de deux, which is a ballet for two people. Scouts from preprofessional programs, schools, and summer intensives showed up from all over the country. That meant there would be people from TSOTA in the audience, which was enough to start a million butterflies swirling inside of my stomach.

Mary Rose had suggested that Jayden and I dance together. She had thought we could impress the judges with some of the lifts you could do with a partner. I couldn't believe it when Jayden agreed. He's the best dancer in our class. With him as my partner, we might have a real shot at getting into the school. And I told myself that when Jayden and I wowed the judges, I'd be so happy that I wouldn't have time to worry about the solo.

At least that's what I hoped.

So here we were, four weeks later, going over our All-City Showcase number and dreaming about being in the newest entering freshman class at Texas School of the Arts.

"I'd never ditch out on my partner," I told Jayden. "Mom was doing some football stuff and running a little late."

"Aww . . . Tanner the Great needed her," Jayden joked, and that's part of why he was the greatest partner ever. He wasn't impressed with my stepbrother either. Partly because his own brother, Malik, played on the team with Tanner. Jayden's dad constantly got on his case about dancing instead of playing sports, especially since Jayden was already six feet tall. But Jayden didn't care; he called himself the LeBron James of ballet and said he was never happier than when he danced.

"Right? Speaking of football, Tanner said that—" But before I could finish, Mary Rose clapped her hands.

"Okay, Jayden and Brooklyn, let's see you run through the Showcase dance."

We took our spots on the floor and the opening notes of Rachmaninoff's Piano Concerto No. 2 in C Minor began. The music was as familiar as breathing. Jayden and I moved across the floor, and once again the world evaporated and I was lost in the dance. When I danced with

Jayden, it was instinct. I didn't need to think; my brain shut off and my muscles remembered every move. He was the perfect partner, never faltering and able to anticipate my every move. His hold on me was sure and firm as I turned into my pirouettes, and I didn't have to worry that he wouldn't be there for me.

The two of us finished with a series of piqué turns and lowered ourselves to the floor. We stayed there as we worked to catch our breath.

Jayden turned toward me.

"Can you see it?" he whispered.

"See what?"

"Our future at Texas School of the Arts. We've got this. We're going to blow those judges away."

I could imagine it. The halls full of people with dance bags, art supplies, and instruments. Days spent studying different artists, rehearsing, and supporting each other as we created new things. Our nights would be busy with student performances, poetry slams, and exhibitions instead of football games. And I'd become so good that Juilliard would beg me to be part of their Summer Dance Intensive.

"Wonderful," Mary Rose said and interrupted my daydream.

"She said we were wonderful," Jayden said and grinned.

"We've got this," I said. Because "wonderful" might

only be one word, but from her, it was the best kind of feedback. Mary Rose had been a principal dancer for the San Francisco Ballet and still danced locally. If something was good in her eyes, you were doing it right, and everyone here strived to get her approval.

She ran through a few other Showcase numbers with students in our class and then ended our usual cool down, but instead of dismissing us to go, Mary Rose asked us all to stay for a minute.

"I need to talk with you about an amazing opportunity we have," she said, and that's when my heart sank because you didn't have to be a mind reader to guess what she was about to say. "We're adding a class to our schedule, so there will be some new guests in the studio."

Maggie groaned. "Please don't tell me it's another tap class. I get such a headache on Wednesdays when they use the room before us. It's nothing but a ton of banging around."

"You mean the toddlers' class? The same one you were once in?" Adeline asked. "I'm pretty sure making a lot of noise is all a group of three-year-olds are good at."

"Whatever, it's still a bunch of racket," Maggie said and rubbed her temples as if the class were happening right now.

"No more tap classes," Mary Rose said. "But this group does have a lot of cheering fans."

I swallowed a giant lump in my throat and pictured Randy, a boy in my biology class who played on the team. A few weeks ago, when we were dissecting frogs, he had thrown an eyeball in the air and it got stuck in the lights. It was the grossest thing ever, but his whole group of football friends thought it was hilarious. So yeah, that's the type of people who will be joining our class.

I wanted my earbuds so I could drown out everything she was saying. Maybe it would go away if I refused to listen. I wished that were the case, but Mary Rose continued to talk about how great this all would be for us.

"Although it sounds somewhat unusual, Leighton Middle School's football team will take conditioning classes here once a week, and I hope you'll give them a warm welcome. This certainly won't be easy for them, so seeing some friendly faces will help."

I glanced around the room and expected to see everyone as outraged as I was to have our studio invaded, and while a few of them looked annoyed or confused, most of my classmates nodded in agreement. Adeline and Elliana were even whispering and smiling, and I saw Maggie and Kirsten high-five each other.

This was awful. My classmates weren't against the idea of the team coming to the studio. In fact, they were excited about it.

I had to do something.

I needed to put a stop to this madness.

I jumped to my feet and spoke up loud enough that everyone could hear me above the excited chatter in the room.

"Aren't you worried about them not taking things seriously?" I asked, because maybe if she knew how much they joked around, she'd reconsider everything. Maybe everyone would.

"Oh, the coach has assured me that they are very serious about this. I've worked with athletes before, and the benefits from dance conditioning are pretty obvious. They're thankful for this chance."

Shoot. That obviously didn't work. I needed to change strategies. Maybe I couldn't stop the classes from happening, but I could try to keep them far away from the studio.

"Wouldn't it make more sense if you held classes at the school? That way the boys wouldn't have to travel all the way here," I said.

"The boys will need to use the barre and mirror to check their positions, so we need to get them into the studio," Mary Rose said.

Into my *studio*, I thought. The one place in Leighton that hadn't been infested by football players. And now it was. And there was nothing I could do about it.

Chapter 7

I rushed out before anyone could see my tears. It was stupid to cry, but I couldn't help it. Ever since we'd moved here, it was as if all the color had drained out of me and I was this black-and-white version of myself. The only time I felt like myself again was at Center Stage Dance Studio. Ballet was all I'd had left that was truly me, and now I'd lost that, too.

I changed as fast as I could, but the other girls came into the dressing room before I was done and the conversation about the football team hadn't stopped.

"Can you believe this news?" Maggie asked, and for a minute, I thought that she was against it. But nope. "This is the greatest thing ever!"

"It's like we won the lottery!" Elliana said and giggled. "I call dibs on the cutest one!"

"Maybe Mary Rose will let them join us in class and we can practice some lifts. Can you imagine anything better?" Adeline asked.

Um, yes, I could. I could imagine a million different things better. You know, like sitting in a bathtub full of cockroaches, having to get a filling without Novocain, or eating ghost peppers. Pretty much anything in the whole entire world was better than the new conditioning classes.

"What do you think, Brooklyn?" Maggie asked.

"Think about what?" Maybe I could play dumb and they'd leave me alone, because it was obvious no one else agreed with my view, so I wasn't about to bring it up in front of all of them.

"About what Mary Rose—"

"Oh wow, look. My phone is ringing. Sorry, I have to take this." I ran out of the room with my phone, which was most definitely not ringing, but they didn't need to know that.

I gave Jayden a quick wave when I passed him in the hall and had almost made it out the door when Mary Rose stepped in front of me.

"Brooklyn! Just the person I was looking for."

"I was about to leave," I said and hoped I didn't sound too rude. I was done. I needed to get home and crawl into my bed and curl up with a bag of peanut butter M&M's and look at puppy videos online.

"I wanted to talk to you about your dance for the All-City Showcase."

"Did it look bad?" I asked, worried she'd tell me I wasn't good enough to get into the school.

"No, not at all. In fact, it's the opposite. You and

Jayden are incredible together, and I think you both have a real shot at getting invited to auditions for TSOTA, not to mention some other offers for summer intensives."

I tried to stay calm so she couldn't see how much I was secretly freaking out inside. She really thought I was that good? Getting into the school was everything. *Please, please, please let that happen.*

"But there's one thing," she said.

My heart sank. There was always a "but," wasn't there?

"While your dancing was stellar and you keep yourself busy with classes, you don't have much else to put on your application."

"What do you mean? I thought my dancing was enough."

"Your dancing will get you noticed at the showcase. But if you get an audition at TSOTA, you also have an interview. You want to stand out when you talk to the school. Jayden volunteers and works with all the younger children in the jazz classes. They want to see that you do things like that too. I thought you could do something out-side of taking classes. And I have the perfect idea."

"Sure, anything," I said, because if Mary Rose could make me well-rounded, then have at it.

"I need someone to help demonstrate all the positions and moves during the conditioning class with the football team. I'll be leading the boys, but I'd love to have you help out by being the model for class. They'll be able to watch what you're doing, which will make things easier. Like when I have the older girls work with your class to help teach new steps. "

"I'm sorry, what?" I asked, because it sounded as if she'd asked me to help with the football team, which I was definitely not okay with.

"Would you want to be a student model in the conditioning class? I thought you'd be perfect for it."

I had no idea what to say. Well, I knew what I *wanted* to say, which was a big fat "no." I didn't want to help. I didn't want anything to do with it. I wanted to stay as far away as I could from that class. But I was pretty sure that wasn't the answer Mary Rose was looking for.

"Like I said, it will look good on your application. It will help you stand out."

Good on my application.

Stand out.

Those were two phrases that meant the world to me. So much, in fact, that I was willing to do anything to make that happen.

Even spend time with the football team.

"Okay, I'd love to," I said. *Love to never see the boys again*, I thought. But I didn't say the rest of the sentence.

How could I? She was giving me a way to look better, and I needed to take it. I needed to do whatever I could to get into that school.

"Great! I was hoping you'd agree. The first class is a week from today. They're going to practice the hour before your technique class."

And just like that, I was the new dance model for the one thing I hated most in the world at that moment. I don't know how things got turned around so quickly, but now, instead of running away from football, I was charging headfirst into it.

Chapter 8

In order to be a dancer, you have to have a high tolerance for pain, especially when you dance on pointe. There's nothing easy about dancing on your toes, and believe me, no one wants to see what my feet look like when I'm rehearsing for a performance. Let's just say I usually avoid sandals for the good of everyone around me.

Dancing was hard, and sometimes I was pretty sure it was near impossible. My muscles ached from the constant beating they got as I tried to master new moves or from pushing my body past the point of exhaustion as I tried to perfect a sequence we had worked on in class. And sure, there were days when I wished I could come home from school and lie around on the couch being lazy or wished I could skip a class to get burritos with Mia, but I loved what I did. When it all seemed like too much, I reminded myself that this is what I'd always dreamed of. I was a dancer. This is the life I wanted. And so I ignored the pain and danced through it.

And that's what I told myself to do as I arrived at the studio to work with the football team.

"Ignore the pain from having those boys here and keep dancing," I told myself.

But as soon as I spotted some of the boys from the middle school team heading into the front door it was as if I had swallowed a rock. A deep feeling settled into my stomach as I thought about how this was real.

The football team was really invading the studio.

I ducked into the changing room and wondered if I could sneak out. There was still time to make a run for it, wasn't there? When Mary Rose asked where I'd gone, I could tell her that I wasn't feeling well or that I'd gotten sick. Which wouldn't even be far from the truth, given the current situation.

But I was a dancer. And a dancer needed to be professional no matter what the situation. Some of the most famous dancers have powered through shows with injuries or family crises happening—a lot worse than having a middle school football team in the studio. If they could do it, so could I. I needed to go out there, volunteer, and get some experience to wow the judges with my whole application.

"Keep your eye on the prize," I told my reflection in the giant mirror that covered one wall of the changing room. "You can handle this and it will all be worth it in the end. Besides, the class is only forty-five minutes long. How bad could it be?"

I took a deep breath, checked to make sure my bun was secure, and headed into the studio.

I entered hesitantly, which wasn't right, because this was the place where I belonged, the place I went when I didn't fit in, so why did I feel like the stranger today?

It was also strange to be in my dance clothes when I was used to being around these boys in jeans and a hoodie. Mary Rose required us to wear proper "ballet attire," as she put it. Girls should be in leotards and tights, and have their hair pinned back. Boys needed to wear dance pants and tank tops.

But I guess the football team didn't get that memo. Or if they did, they ignored it, because the boys were dressed as if they were going out on the field to practice, in shorts or baggy athletic pants that make swishing noises when you take a step. They had on T-shirts and hooded sweatshirts, and everyone wore sneakers.

I didn't feel like I belonged, even though I was the one who'd worn the right thing, which made no sense at all. It was like that first day of living in Tanner's house all over again. When the movers had left and it was only the four of us, Stephen had told us to make ourselves at home, but I hadn't known what to do, because it wasn't our home.

I stood at the entrance of the room. No one said anything for a moment, and I had no idea. Usually, we started at the barre, but no one else was there. The boys were in a group in the middle of the room, so it was odd to walk over to the barre. Mary Rose was by the speakers, but to get there, I had to cross in front of everyone, so instead, I stood like a deer caught in the headlights, waiting and wondering what the heck I was supposed to do. *Why didn't I make a run for it when I had the chance?*

I shifted my weight from one foot to the other and the floor creaked. Randy glanced my way.

"Um, since when do girls play football?" he called out. I didn't know all the boys yet, since I'd only been to Leighton Middle School for a few months, but I knew Randy. He was hard to miss. He was in a few of my classes and was the type of kid who always yelled things out in the middle of class when our teacher was talking. What a surprise, he was doing it here, too. I guess I shouldn't have expected anything different when the boys entered this class.

"I *don't* play football," I told him and made sure to make it clear exactly how I felt about the silly sport. "In fact, I don't even *watch* football. But I hear your team is really stinking up the place. So I'm here to help you guys so you can maybe try to win a game or two."

"Oh, burn!" another boy named Jimmy said. A few of the boys whooped and hollered, and one even clapped at my comeback, but Randy's eyes narrowed and he clenched his jaw. Before he could do anything in retaliation, Mary Rose clapped her hands together.

"Okay, that's enough. We're here to learn the fundamentals of dance so you can keep yourself safe on the field and hopefully move a little faster when the other team is chasing you. Winning is just a plus," she said and smiled in that way that made everyone like her. Mary Rose was supertiny; she wasn't even five feet tall and wore her hair in two braids that she pinned around her head like a crown. She was pretty much a real, live fairy princess, and I could easily imagine her dancing in *A Midsummer Night's Dream*, one of my favorite ballets of all time. She took dance seriously, and when you were in her studio, you were there to work and she didn't tolerate anything otherwise, but she always added a playful touch by wearing fun-colored leg warmers with her leotards. Today, she had on one red leg warmer and one white: LHS colors.

Ugh. She better not be infected with Leighton football fever too.

"Brooklyn, why don't you come up front by me?" she asked, and I relaxed a tiny bit, relieved to know what to do. I stepped up alongside of her, and she placed an arm around my shoulder and gave me a little hug. "Class, say hello to our helper, Brooklyn. She's one of our best dancers at the studio, and she's going to work alongside you to provide an example for how to do things in the correct way."

"Really? We need someone to show us how to spin in circles?" Randy asked. The boy would not quit. "If that's the case, I think we're in more trouble than Coach Konarski thought."

"That's enough," Mary Rose said and gave him her trademark look. The one that stopped anyone in their tracks from goofing around or talking back. And just like clockwork, Randy shut his mouth and shrank back into his group of friends.

I didn't even bother spending a moment getting mad at how idiotic he sounded. Instead, I held on to what Mary Rose had said.

One of her best students.

My cheeks warmed with pride, and I imagined myself sharing the news with her when I got into TSOTA. She'd probably jump up and let out when of those little squeals she does whenever something really good happens. She'd be so proud of me, and I'd thank her for everything she'd done to help me get in. It would be amazing. Correction. It *will* be amazing. I *will* get into that school. But first, I had to survive class with these boys.

I gave the group a small wave and made sure to look right at Randy. *You may be good at football*, I thought, *but I'm the one who knows what I'm doing here.*

"Okay," Mary Rose said. "Let's start by doing some warm-ups at the barre. Grab a spot there while I get the music going. Brooklyn will stand at the front and demonstrate for you. Follow her lead."

The boys moved over to the barre without complaining, but it was what some of them did after they got there that solidified my original idea that they weren't going to take any part of this seriously.

A few of the boys swung off of the barre and made monkey noises as if they were in the jungle instead of class. They scratched their armpits and jumped around and acted like they were raised, well, in the wild.

It was horrible. Not to mention superdangerous. They could hurt themselves, or the barre could come loose. Seriously, how immature do you have to be to act like that?

"Hold up a minute," a voice boomed across the room.

Mary Rose. The boys froze, surprised to see so much power coming out of such a tiny person.

"This will stop right now. I refuse to tolerate any behavior like this in my studio." She stood in the center of the room and gave each and every one of the boys the same look she'd given Randy minutes ago. I waited to see what she'd do. If we tried anything like that during class, she would kick us right out. And I know that for a fact because once when we were working on a piece from *Swan Lake*, Adeline waved her arms up and down and made giant honking noises like she was one of the swans in the lake by our school. Mary Rose told her to leave until she was able to get herself together and take dance seriously. "You have about ten seconds to decide if you want to stay here and respect this place or leave. I fully intend to inform your coach about your use of class time here, and I hope that I can say it's been a positive one. Can I count on that?"

The boys nodded and it seemed as if they were afraid of Mary Rose. Or at least her threat to talk to their coach.

"Good. Now let's get moving. We're going to loosen ourselves up, so follow what Brooklyn is doing."

I led the boys through our usual warm-ups and not one of them grumbled and complained. Well, none of them but Randy. I don't know what his problem was, but it was clear that he didn't want to be there.

"Is this all there is?" he muttered when Mary Rose was putting a new song on. "I mean, this is hardly a workout. I do more when I'm volunteering at my grandpa's retirement home."

"Really?" I snapped, fed up with him. Mary Rose may have asked me to help with the class, but she never said anything about being nice to them. "You think this is easy? How about you try this?"

I backed up so I was at one end of the room and launched into la seconde turns. I spun around and around and got that rush of pure adrenaline I loved so much. When I finished, I leaned against the wall and my heart raced from both the exertion and nerves of dancing in front of these boys.

"Can your grandpa do that, Randy?" I asked. And when he didn't answer, I smiled smugly. "I thought so."

I glanced at the group. Most stood with their mouths open as if I'd scored the game-winning touchdown, and it kind of, sort of felt like I had.

Chapter 9

The rest of the class went by without any incidents. The boys listened to what Mary Rose said and actually weren't bad at some of the stuff, even if she did change the wording of a few of the techniques to football terms, which to me seemed an awful lot like disrespecting the art of ballet. But Mary Rose knew what she was doing, and I, for one, respected that.

She would ask me to do a specific ballet technique, but then when it was time for the boys to try it, she'd change the name to something that had to do with football. The demi plié became the position you get in to play defense and a relevé was how you went up to catch the football.

"See how Brooklyn is stretching her leg up high like that? You want to pull back like you're about to kick a field goal." She turned toward me. "Brooklyn, can you show them how to do that again?"

"You mean how to do an arabesque?" I asked, because the boys should know what it was actually called. It wasn't like I was turning their football terms into ballet ones.

The only ray of light in all of this was that at the end of class I overheard two of the boys talking.

"This wasn't as easy as I thought," Jimmy told another boy named Logan, who nodded in agreement.

"It was an actual workout," Logan said, and instantly I liked him for acknowledging that ballet wasn't easy. It was work. Hard work.

Instead of rushing out of the studio, I stayed in the room. Mary Rose always had a cup of tea between classes, so the room was mine. I put on music from *The Sleeping Beauty* and threw myself into the Fairies Variation. I didn't think about football, or the middle school boys, or Tanner, or Stephen, or even Mom. All I thought about was the dance and the world I was now lost in. I danced without thinking. I let the motions take over, and everything else fell away.

When I was young, I used to jump into the swimming pool at Grandma's apartment complex and sit underwater for as long as I could. I loved how the world would go silent and the sounds became muffled and blocked out. It was like that with dance, too. When it was just me, it was as if I was in a trance where the only thing I heard was the music and the rest of my brain went blank. It was sitting deep underwater in that swimming pool, and what went on in the outside world was whooshed away and gone.

When I was done, I sprawled out on the floor and tried to catch my breath. I glanced at the clock and was surprised to see that class had started five minutes ago.

There were only one girl from my class here, and usually most of us arrived early to do our own warm-ups so we could get right into dancing.

"What's going on?" I asked her.

Corrine gestured to the lobby, annoyed. "The boy's football team is what's going on. The rest of the class has pretty much lost their minds about them being here."

"And you haven't?" I asked her, and when she shook her head no, I was so glad that I wasn't the only one who didn't welcome the boys here with open arms.

I headed out to the lobby to investigate and Corrine was right. Beyond a few girls who stood off to the side and looked too shy to talk to the team, everyone else was crowded around them. It sounded as if Center Stage had been invaded by giggles. Tons of them, loud and high-pitched.

Maggie and Elliana jumped up and down and moved their hands around in big, dramatic motions as they told some story to a group of boys.

Adeline laughed hysterically at something Randy was saying, something I'm sure wasn't funny at all.

Even Jayden was there, talking to some of the boys on the team about a teacher at our school.

This was bad. Very bad, and called for drastic action. I needed to take back my studio and end this madness before my friends forgot why they came to Center Stage. The girls were simply caught up in the spell of football, hypnotized like the rest of the town, and it was up to me to save them.

I cleared my throat—the loud, obnoxious way that teachers do when you're talking and they want you to be quiet.

A few people glanced in my direction but then turned back and continued to carry on as if everyone was the best of friends.

I cleared my throat again even louder and clapped my hands together like Mary Rose does to start class.

"I don't know about all of you, but I'm ready to get to class," I announced.

"Funny, because I was about to say that I'm ready to get some pizza," Randy said, and the girls laughed as if that was the funniest joke in the world.

News flash—it wasn't.

I grabbed Adeline's arm and pulled her with me, but she shook it off.

"It's time for class," I told her.

"Geez, relax, we're welcoming the new students. Mary Rose wanted us to make them feel like they belong."

"Are you wearing makeup?" I asked, even though it was obvious. Adeline had on bright red lipstick and a little too much blush on her cheeks. I know for a fact that she isn't allowed to wear makeup, because her mom always makes her wipe it off right after a performance.

"A little. Is there something wrong with that?" she asked, and I thought maybe I was living in some kind of alternate universe where things didn't make sense. A world where all my friends suddenly couldn't care less about ballet and had turned boy crazy. That had to be the case. My friends couldn't have turned this boy crazy so fast, right?

"Yeah, why don't you go back into the classroom and twirl some more?" Randy spoke up. And I thought I was going to cry. And not a little sniffle, but a full-out sob fest, complete with a snotty nose and tons of tissues. Because this so wasn't right and no one could see it but me. My lip trembled like it does before the tears fall, and I didn't think I could keep it together. But as I was about to fall apart, Jayden spoke up.

"Brooklyn is right; it's time break this huddle up. We have new steps to learn, and I'm pretty sure you boys have football plays to memorize."

I don't know how he did it, but the group moved toward the door and said their good-byes. The dancers moved toward the studio and the team headed outside.

"I have no idea what kind of magic that was, but you saved the day," I told Jayden.

Jayden took an exaggerated deep bow. "Of course. Anything for my amazing dance partner. And the secret is to talk in a language they understand. I learned that from my brother a long time ago."

"Yeah, Mary Rose seems to think the same thing. You two might be on to something, and in this case, you knew just the right thing to say, so thanks."

"It's all in a day's work," Jayden said. "And now, I don't know about you, but someone said it was time to start class, so that's exactly what I plan to do."

I followed him into the room with a grin on my face because life was back to normal, and it was exactly the way it was supposed to be.

The girls settled down and, thankfully, there was no mention of the boys. I threw myself into the movements, and we danced for over an hour without stopping. No one complained or goofed off or tried to make it into a big joke. In fact, it was the opposite. Jayden and I went over our piece for the Showcase and did such a good job that the rest of the class gave us a round of applause at the end.

"Dance like that at the All-City Showcase, and you are both sure to catch the recruiter's eye for one of the six spots that are open at TSOTA," Mary Rose said as she clapped along with everyone else.

"Six spots?" I asked.

Mary Rose nodded. "I got word that they're only taking six dancers this year. They took twelve last year, but said they wanted to keep the group a bit smaller. You have nothing to worry about, though. I have confidence both of you will take two of those spots. You're doing amazing things with the choreography, and your lifts are perfection."

I really wish I could have focused on the good things Mary Rose was saying, but it was impossible not to worry. How could I not when there were only six spots? Half of what they'd had the year before. That meant competition would be even tougher.

Jayden and I were the only ones from our studio trying to get into TSOTA, but how many other kids wanted a spot? For all I knew, it could be hundreds. The school was open to anyone from the entire state. Some students even traveled over an hour each way every day to get there. After all, if you loved to dance, why wouldn't you want to go to a school where you got to do that for half the day?

Six spots meant I really had to stand out at the Showcase and on my application. In a matter of minutes, my chances of getting into TSOTA seemed to have gotten a lot harder, which meant that I needed every advantage I could get. Translation: I had to continue to volunteer with the football team. There was no way I could escape them.

Chapter 10

Tanner was waiting outside in his truck for me after practice. Mom and Stephen had made a deal with him that they would buy him a used truck if he helped with taking me to and from my classes when Mom or Stephen couldn't. That seemed like a pretty great deal. For Tanner. I, on the other hand, was held hostage in a truck that usually smelled like a locker room and had to listen to him talk football, football, football.

Today when I climbed in, he was watching a football video on his phone.

"Check out the size of the guys on the team we're playing next week. They're beasts," he told me and turned the screen so I could see too.

"Wow, they're huge," I said to try to be polite, even though the last thing I wanted right now was to hear more about football.

"I know. I'm usually not nervous about a game, but these guys are going to make us work for a win."

I eyed him suspiciously. "Wait a minute, should I call

all of the news stations? Is Tanner Kratus really saying that he's nervous about a game?"

"Contrary to popular belief, it isn't always as easy as I make it look," he joked as he pulled out of the parking lot. "Speaking of football players. How did the middle school team do today? Coach Trentanelli mentioned that they were going to start working at the studio."

"Well, I wouldn't exactly call what they did 'work.'" I thought about Randy and how awful he was.

"Are they not taking it seriously? Because I'll let Coach know right away."

"No, no," I said quickly. I didn't want the team at my studio, but I wasn't about to get them in trouble.

"This will be good for them," Tanner said. "They need this."

"What about me? What do I get out of this?"

"You get to be the one who single-handedly saved Leighton football."

"Um, what?"

"You're our city's last hope. Only you can fix the team and get them straightened out, or we're doomed. You hold the power, Brooklyn," he said jokingly, like I was some sort of football superhero.

"Well, when you put it that way . . ."

"Right now you're the most important person in the

entire town. Don't let us down. All hope depends on you."

"Okay, now you're taking it a little too far," I said, but I had to admit it was pretty funny. Who would have thought that ballet was what would save our football team?

"I'm serious," he insisted. "You're the chosen one. Can you do it?"

"It's going to be hard, but I'm up for the challenge." I said, playing along. I wrinkled my nose as I thought about Randy. "Well, there are a few obstacles in the way, but no pain, no gain, right?"

"Exactly. Thanks again for your service," Tanner said.

"Anytime," I said. And while it didn't fix the problem of having the team at the studio, it was fun to joke with Tanner.

Chapter 11

Mia got to lunch early the next day and nabbed one of the best tables by the windows that faced the outside playing fields. When you're stuck at school for seven hours a day, there is nothing better than being able to look outside. And as a bonus, this table was near the end of the lunch line, where they put out the desserts. Mia loved that she could see the exact moment the chocolate chip cookies were out and grab one while they were still hot and gooey.

She waved me over, no doubt dying to hear all about the football team at the dance studio. Sure enough, she didn't even let me get a word in before I sat down.

"I can't believe my mom wouldn't let me text you last night," Mia complained. "She's so unfair."

"She never lets you text me after eight p.m.," I reminded her. Mia's mom firmly believed that nothing good happened with technology in the evening hours. She didn't want Mia stimulated by the screen and most certainly didn't want her texting late into the night, so Mia had to hand over her phone and didn't get it back until the morning. It usually wasn't that big a deal to me, since after I got home from dance classes I ate, finished my homework, showered, and fell into bed from exhaustion, but sometimes there were those moments like last night when you needed to talk to your BFF and you couldn't. And those moments were the worst.

"I told her it was a life-or-death situation, but she wouldn't budge." Mia picked the pepperonis off her slice of pizza and popped them into her mouth one by one.

"Parents just don't understand," I said in solidarity, thinking about Mom, who hadn't come home from work last night until late, and when she had, she hadn't even asked how class with the team had gone.

"You've got that right. But we're together now, so spill it. I need the scoop on the class. Was it everything you thought it would be and more?"

"It wasn't as bad as I thought it would be. Most of them actually took it pretty seriously, but still. That's my space. I hated having the team invade it."

"Could you avoid them? Pretend they aren't there? You could tell your teacher you don't want to help with them." Mia was always telling me that life is too short to do something you don't want to do.

"I wish," I said. "But I have to. The competition is really tough for TSOTA this year. Only six people are going to get into the freshman class, so I need to make sure my application stands out."

"I have a solution to that," Mia said. "You could go to Leighton High School with me. You don't have to go to Texas School of the Arts."

"But I want to go there. More than anything," I said.

"More than going to school with your best friend. We just found each other and now you're already planning on leaving me," Mia said in a half-joking, half-serious way that always made me get that awful tug in my stomach whenever we talked about this. I hated that going to TSOTA meant not being with Mia, and I understood why she was upset, but ballet was my passion. It was where I was the most like myself. Where I belonged.

"It's not about leaving you," I told her for the millionth time. "It's about doing what I love. And we'll still see each other. We can have weekly breakfast dates at Locos Tacos and sleepovers every weekend. You might not see me around school, but you'll be so sick of seeing me so much outside of school that it won't matter."

"It won't be the same." Mia sighed, and I couldn't help but agree. She was my first friend here, and it stunk to think that I might separate the two of us. But she had to understand why I wanted to go to that school so bad; it was the same as her drive to become a sportscaster and why she did her vlog.

"What if we start a Web series where we make videos for each other? We could post them every day," I suggested, and Mia perked up a bit.

"That would be so cool! Like virtual pen pals!"

The idea did sound fun and something I could totally see us doing. We were about to launch into a planning session about how it would work when there was a ton of noise from the front of the cafeteria.

A group of boys had entered, tossing a football back and forth and acting as if they owned the place.

"Are you kidding me?" I asked. "Even when I try to get away from the team, it's impossible. It's like they're lurking around every corner waiting to jump out at me."

"That's a bit much," Mia said. "My guess is they're here to eat lunch."

"Well, they don't need to make a racket about it," I told her and pointed at the football. "Besides, that's so dangerous. I can't believe no one is stopping them."

Mia rolled her eyes. "Okay, cafeteria cop. Lighten up. What's the worst that could happen? Someone gets hit with the football?"

"Um, they could poke an eye out, break someone's

nose, knock one of the cafeteria monitors down, give you a concussion—"

Mia held up her hand at me to stop and shook her head as if she couldn't believe how ridiculous I truly was, which, okay, maybe I *was* being a little over-the-top.

The boys continued to make their way through the tables as they tossed the ball around. I waited for one of the adults to say something, but instead, my classmates clapped and cheered them on.

"This is a bad dream, right?" I asked when the boys sat at the table right next to us. Suddenly, our awesome table by the windows turned into the worst table in the cafeteria. In fact, I'd rather be at the dreaded table next to the line of garbage cans than stay here.

"Let's sit somewhere else," I told Mia and stood up. I began to gather my stuff, but she placed her hand on my tray.

"You're being ridiculous. We're staying here. Ignore them. Besides, I need to eavesdrop and see if I can get the scoop for my next vlog."

I reluctantly sat down. The boys had pulled out their lunches and were debating who had the best food and what kind of swaps could be made.

"Do you think I can record them on my phone?" Mia whispered.

"What's there to record? Right now, their conversation

pretty much revolves around the best flavor of Doritos."

"Cool Ranch," Mia said without missing a beat. "Definitely Cool Ranch."

"You're hopeless," I told her.

I tried my best to tune out the group and focus on my lunch, which was a giant salad with quinoa and sunflower seeds on it. I thought I'd done a good job at ignoring the boys until I heard the word "ballet."

"Turn on your recorder," I said to Mia. "Quick!"

"Oh, I see how it is. Now, when you want it, it's suddenly okay," she said, but recorded them nonetheless. "What are they talking about?"

"Ballet," I said and held my finger to my lips to get her to be quiet. I needed to hear the conversation.

Randy turned to Jimmy. "Did your mom buy you a tutu yet for class? I think pink will look good on you."

I bit my lip to keep from saying anything. What a ridiculous question! You don't even wear a tutu to class. In fact, there were tons of ballets where no one wore them at all. What he was saying was a big, huge stereotype repeated by people who didn't know anything about the world of dance, but Jimmy didn't seem to care. He laughed as if Randy had said the funniest thing in the world.

"I can't believe Coach is making us go back," Randy complained.

"It's pretty dumb," Anthony agreed, which stung a bit because at practice, he'd been into things and I'd thought he wasn't that bad. "Like, we could be doing much more important things on the field."

"I'm pretty sure Coach Konarski knows what he's doing. After all, the Cowboys use ballet as part of their training," Logan said. I thought back to how he had said ballet was hard work and was thankful again for his support.

"I don't care who does it; it's a waste of our time," Randy argued.

Mia listened to them as if they were having the most fascinating conversation in the world. I, on the other hand, could hardly sit still. With each silly comment Randy and some of the other boys on the team made, I got angrier and angrier, and I was pretty sure if you took my temperature, it would show that my blood had reached a boiling point. I grabbed the edge of the table so hard my knuckles were white.

"Ignore him. He's being stupid," Mia told me, which was easy for her to say. I bet she'd get upset if he made fun of her vlogs.

"I can't," I told her. "Mary Rose let him come into the studio; the least he could do is respect that."

I pushed my chair back with so much force that it fell to the floor. But I didn't care. I stormed over to their table and stopped at the head of it with my hands on my hips. It was all very angry and dramatic, but no one noticed me at first.

"Could you please be quiet for one minute?" I shouted and banged my fist down on the table. I did it so hard a few of the trays rattled and everyone stopped talking.

"Geez, calm down, twinkle toes," Randy said, which made me even more mad.

"My name is Brooklyn," I told him and gave him the meanest look I could muster. "Listen up, because I'm only going to say this once. No one asked you to come to our studio. I didn't *want* you to come to our studio. But you did! You showed up smelling like dirty old gym socks and making jokes out of everything. Well, guess what? Ballet isn't a joke. Not one little bit. How would you feel if I showed up on the football field when you were trying to practice and made fun of everything you did?"

The boys simply sat there with their eyes on me and mouths hanging open. It felt good to tell them exactly what I thought, so I continued with my tirade.

"If you don't want to come to class, don't, because no one wants you there! Do us all a favor and stay home!"

I was out of breath and my heart raced, almost as if I had finished an intense dance routine, but it felt good. It was amazing to tell Randy exactly what I thought about how rude he'd been at my studio. And to his credit, he simply stared at me for a moment and I thought I'd finally, finally, gotten through to him.

But then he began to laugh. It was loud and echoing, and other people in the cafeteria turned to see what the fuss was about.

"What we do on the field is so different from what you do in the studio, you wouldn't be able to last a minute," he said.

"You're delusional. You have no idea how much harder dancers work than you," I snapped and threw my hands up in the air. I gave up. Randy was terrible. There was no getting through their thick football-filled skulls.

I marched back to my table and threw myself in the chair. I made sure to keep my back to the team so I wouldn't have to look at any of them.

"I'm done!" I told Mia. "Totally done with Leighton football."

"Um, yeah, I think we heard that loud and clear," she said and set her phone down. She slid it toward me. "Press play."

I did and my whole freak-out replayed before me on her phone. As I watched the video, my eyes narrowed in on Randy.

Any time I wasn't facing him, he mimicked what I was doing with large, exaggerated actions.

He was awful.

The whole idea of having the team at Center Stage was awful, awful, awful.

And the worst part was, there was no escaping them. If I wanted to go to TSOTA, I was stuck with them for the entire season. There was no way out of this.

Chapter 12

I became a social media sensation.

During the next two days, the video of me yelling at Randy and the other boys had gotten more hits than anything Mia had ever posted.

I was pretty sure that every single person living in Leighton, Texas, had seen it. And I wouldn't be surprised if everyone in the surrounding cities watched it too.

"Take that video down," I told Mia. "It makes me look like a crazy person."

"You kind of were," Mia said. "But now you're Internet famous. That's a big deal!"

"Yeah, famous for going nuts at the football team," I told her. Usually, I was cool with her posting whatever she wanted because of art and free speech and creative expression and all that, but this was a bit extreme. Classmates stopped me in the hallway and made comments about the video, and an older girl even recognized me when I was picking up Chinese food with Mom.

"Seriously," I pleaded with her. "Take it down."

"I can't," Mia said. "It's gotten over a thousand hits. That's huge. This may be my best video yet."

"You didn't do anything. I did. And I look ridiculous."

"Come on, look on the bright side. It's getting people's attention. Maybe it will catch the eye of one of the judges at your dance school."

"And what? They give me a spot at the school based on my amazing talent of freaking out?"

Before she could answer, my phone buzzed and Jayden's name popped up on my screen.

"Mia, I have to go. Jayden's on the other line. Take down that video, because I promise, if you don't, I'll tell everyone you still sleep with a night-light."

"You wouldn't!"

"Try me. I don't think you want to mess with me. You have video proof of how mad I get when someone upsets me."

"Good point," she said. "I'll delete it."

I said a quick good-bye and switched over to Jayden's call. He had been at his cousin Raja's house all day, and I was pretty sure he'd fill me in on the latest dance moves she taught him. She was a cheerleader, and the two of them taught each other their dance routines. At least he wouldn't talk about football. Jayden was the one person

I could count on not to go all football crazy.

"What's up?" I asked. "How was your cousin's house?"

"It was okay, but . . . ," he said and then trailed off.

"But what?"

"But then it wasn't."

"It wasn't? Why not?" I asked, confused. Jayden loved hanging out with Raja.

"Promise you won't hate me?"

"You're not making sense. Of course I won't hate you. Unless, of course, you tell me you joined the football team."

"It's worse," he said, but how could anything be worse than that? "I broke my leg."

Yep. It was worse.

"You're joking, right?"

"I was spotting Raja on a lift, and she lost her balance. I tried to stop her from falling, but instead, we both went down. When I hit the floor, my leg made this gross snapping noise. You should've heard it. It was like a tree branch. Really—"

"Stop! Too much information," I told him, because *yuck*. I didn't need to know every gory detail.

"All I have to say is it was really gross and now I have a giant cast on my leg."

"Wait, what? A giant cast?" I was so busy trying not to listen to Jayden's description of the fall that I didn't even think about what had happened.

"Yeah, it goes all the way up to my knee. I need crutches to get around."

"How long do you have to wear it?"

"A long time," he quietly said.

"How long?" I asked, and when Jayden didn't answer right away, I knew this was going to be bad.

"Six to eight weeks," he said. "And then I have to do physical therapy and can't dance for at least another month."

"But the Showcase is in three months," I said, which before sounded so far away but now with Jayden's injury was way too soon. A rising sense of panic began to build in me.

"It's awful," he said. "It was such a stupid thing to do, and I ruined my chances of getting into the school."

I paused before I let my panic take over and tried to put myself in Jayden's place. It's not like he meant for this to happen. He wasn't just my dance partner; he was my friend, and he had been there for me a lot in the past. Now it was my turn to be there for him.

"How are you feeling?" I asked. "Does it hurt?"

"A little," he admitted. "But I can handle the pain. It's missing out on the Showcase that hurts."

"While I'm glad your leg doesn't hurt, it stinks that we won't be able to dance together," I told him. "But don't worry about anything. Please change to a period. Just get better. I'll figure something out."

"But you can still dance in the Showcase with your solo," Jayden said. "You're a great dancer. You can easily get into the school dancing by yourself."

That was where he was wrong. Maybe I *used* to be a good dancer, but that was in the past. The idea of dancing a solo, and only a solo, terrified me.

"We're a great *team*," I said. "And now it's just me."

"I'm sorry, Brooklyn. You have to know that I really didn't mean for this to happen. I had my heart set on getting into TSOTA too," he said one more time, and I couldn't very well be mad at him for an accident. Especially when his chances of getting into the school were also ruined.

"It's okay," I told him.

But it wasn't. Not even close.

Chapter 13

I hung up with Jayden and headed to the kitchen. Mom would be in there making dinner. She had a way of making everything better simply by talking with me, and I most definitely needed to make things better.

I turned the corner to the kitchen ready for a full dose of Mom love, but when I walked in, she wasn't the only one there and there was no sign of dinner. Instead, she sat at the table with Stephen and Tanner.

Tanner had his head in his hands, and Mom's hand was on his back. Had something happened? Maybe we could eat ice cream and be miserable together. Misery loved company, right?

"Hi, Brooklyn. We were about to call you down. You must have read our minds," Mom said when she saw me. She patted the empty seat by her. "Why don't you join us? We have something to tell you."

Tanner lifted his head, and I gave him one of those half smiles to show him that I understood what he was going through. That I was having a bad day too.

"Is everything okay?" I asked him.

"I got some news earlier that doesn't quite seem real."

"Me too," I told him in solidarity. "There's nothing worse than bad news."

"Oh, this isn't bad," Tanner said. "It's the opposite."

"That's right!" Stephen chimed in. "Everything is fine. In fact, everything is amazing!"

Speak for yourself, I thought, and another wave of sadness washed over me as I thought about Jayden.

"Tanner is going to be the newest player on the University of Texas football team! He was just offered a scholarship to play for them!" Stephen burst out as if he couldn't hold the news in any longer, and you would've thought Tanner had figured out how to make world peace happen from how excited Stephen was.

Mom jumped up from her seat and danced around the kitchen. Tanner looked a little embarrassed at how our parents were acting, but also pretty excited.

I, on the other hand, felt as if I'd been punched in the stomach and then thrown into an ice-cold swimming pool. Tanner got a football scholarship? For college? How unfair could life be at the moment? This was the kind of news I had wished and hoped to get after the Showcase. Instead, I'd found out the opposite only moments ago. I wasn't going to be going anywhere next year, while Tanner got into one of the best football schools in the state.

"Isn't this great?" Mom asked when I didn't respond.

"Yeah, great," I replied in a daze.

"It hasn't sunk in. I got a full ride to the University of Texas. They made the offer today. It's like I'm dreaming," he said.

More like having a nightmare, I thought, but then felt bad. Tanner deserved this. It's just, did I really need to find out about this right after I got the awful news from Jayden?

"Oh, it's a dream," Stephen said and patted Tanner on the back. "You earned that scholarship. You worked hard for it."

"And we definitely need to celebrate!" Mom said. She pointed at the box of pasta sitting on the counter and wrinkled her nose. "Who wants to eat boring old spaghetti when we've got news like this? Let's go out! What do you think, Tanner? Where do you want to go?"

Tanner suggested our favorite barbeque place, and the three of them continued to have a conversation about how great Tanner was and the incredible news and blah, blah, blah. I didn't want to hear it. Maybe I was acting like a poor sport and I should've been excited for him, but how could I be when what was happening to him was exactly what I'd been dreaming would happen to me with TSOTA? And now that dream was crushed.

"And think, Brooklyn," Mom said in a superhappy

voice, "once you get into Texas School of the Arts, we'll be celebrating that, too!"

I didn't have the heart to tell her that wasn't going to happen anymore, which made everything a million times worse than it already was.

"What a household full of talented kids we have!" Stephen added. "I think we may have the two most talented kids in the entire state of Texas!"

"One," I whispered to myself. Tanner was the only talented one. And what stunk the worst was that the best day of his life was the worst day of mine.

Chapter 14

ayden showed up to math class the next day with a lime-green cast. Elliana and Adeline stood on either side of him like body guards.

"We're Jayden's official bag carriers," Elliana said, and Adeline spun around to show me that she had Jayden's giant red backpack on. "We take the job very seriously."

"Especially because we can leave class five minutes early and take our time to get to his next class," Adeline said, and Elliana rolled her eyes.

"Some of us like to be late for class," Elliana said, and pointedly looked at Adeline. "The rest of us value our education."

"Oh, I do," Adeline said. "I take lunch and gym class very seriously."

I couldn't help but laugh, even though this was nothing new. The two of them fought like sisters. They were always arguing about something, and it was usually silly. I tuned out their conversation and turned toward Jayden.

"I have a special get well present for you," I said. Jayden was such a good friend, and I felt guilty about how upset

I was when he told me about his foot. I handed him a gift bag that I'd stuffed some tissue paper into.

"You didn't need to get me anything," he said, but I nodded toward it.

"It's just something little. Open it up."

Jayden pulled out a long stick with prongs on the end. "What is this?"

"Trust me, you'll be thanking me. I heard that it can get pretty itchy inside that cast, and since you have to wear it for so long . . ."

Jayden groaned. "Don't remind me."

"Speaking of your cast," I said and gestured toward it. "You should've picked a brighter color. I can't see it."

"Hey, go big or go home," Jayden said, and I couldn't argue with that. That's the way Jayden was. When he walked in the room, he somehow managed to be the life of the party. People noticed him. Maggie had once said that was part of his magic onstage, that the audience wanted to watch him, and it was true. Jayden was one of those people who seemed to have been born a star, and whatever it was he had, I was lucky to have been a part of it when he agreed to dance with me.

"Are you sure you can't be a part of the Showcase?" I asked. "Your injury doesn't look too bad."

"You're right. Maybe we could change things around, and you could lift me instead."

"It would definitely get the judges' attention," I said.

Jayden's face grew serious. "Listen, I really am sorry for what happened."

I dismissed him with my hand. Talking about this wouldn't change anything. It was now my job to make Jayden feel better. "It's okay, you don't have to apologize. It was an accident."

"Maybe Mary Rose can find you another partner?" he suggested. "Or you could see if you could just dance your solo."

"Yeah, I don't know about that . . . ," I started and then trailed off. Because how do I explain how hard it is to just rely on my solo?

"Or you could join drill team with us!" Elliana said, which was something she'd begged me to do multiple times. Drill team was the reason the two of them weren't taking part in the All-City Showcase. The team performed at all the Leighton High football games, and the reason the two of them took classes at Center Stage in the first place was so they had a chance to get on the team. It was almost as impossible to earn a spot as it was to get into TSOTA, but Elliana and Adeline were determined to do it. I was pretty sure they'd make the team too; those two could dance.

"I don't think I could ever trade in my ballet slippers for the drill team boots," I said.

"But they're amazing," Elliana exclaimed, and clutched her hands to her heart and swooned.

She was right about that. They wore white cowboy boots with fringe on them and silver spurs on the backs that sparkled under the stadium lights. They were pretty cool. But those boots had nothing on my shoes. I thought about all my pairs of beat-up pointe shoes. The stiff leather you have to break in. The cracked bottoms and split heels worn from hours of dancing on them. The cool satin ribbon against my fingers as I laced myself in. Sometimes I thought I was more comfortable in my pointe shoes than regular shoes.

I lifted my foot behind me and did an arabesque. There was a gentle tug in my calf muscles, and I smiled at the familiar pull. Ballet was what I wanted. It was as important to me as breathing.

"Nope, I think I'm perfectly fine in my slippers," I told them and glanced at Jayden. "But it looks like I may just dance at Center Stage for now. I don't think I could be in the Showcase without my right-hand man."

The bell for class rang saving me from any other questions that Elliana and Adeline might have.

"We have to get moving or we're going to be late," Elliana said.

Adeline dismissed her with a swipe of her hand. "No worries, remember? We have an excuse."

"Glad to see that my tragedy is your personal gain," Jayden said. "And since you're taking your sweet time getting to class, do you think that you could get me a breakfast sandwich from the cafeteria first?"

"I don't think we can work that much magic with the broken leg excuse," Elliana said and turned to Adeline. "I do need to get to class. Some of us want to be there on time."

"Yeah, yeah, yeah," Adeline said and held out Jayden's bag to me. "Can you help him to his next class?"

"You trust me to be his bodyguard?" I asked.

"You're the only person we'd trust," Adeline solemnly said.

"I'm honored," I said and waved good-bye as they raced off to class.

"Those two," I said and laughed one more time. I dug around in my book bag until I found the Sharpie I used to write my name on stuff for ballet so it wouldn't get lost in the changing room. I held it up to Jayden. "And on that note, we have important things to do. Let me sign that cast of yours."

"Make sure you sign it nice and big. After all, your autograph is going to be worth something someday," Jayden said.

"Both our autographs are going to be worth something," I corrected him.

"I like the sound of that," he said as I bent down and signed my name with a flourish on his cast.

Chapter 15

The following week at school, you would've thought my family won the lottery the way they were acting about the news of Tanner's scholarship. Mom and Stephen wore their UT sweatshirts all weekend and the cheerleaders came and decorated our front yard for Tanner. It was all anyone talked about all day, so when I got home that afternoon, I half expected to see Tanner on the TV. I wouldn't be surprised if the national news covered it. It felt like these days anything was possible, no matter how outrageous it seemed.

The only positive about all of this craziness was that Tanner and Stephen had made the short drive to Austin to visit the University of Texas for the day to talk with some of the coaches and walk around the campus, so I had Mom all to myself. She'd be home soon from the job she'd gotten when we moved here. She was secretary at an elementary school in the next town over. I bet even her school had heard all about the amazing Tanner and his scholarship.

I dropped my book bag off in the family room and headed toward the kitchen. The plan was to make some of our favorite tea from Oregon, which Dasha had surprised me with in a care package, and then have a heart-to-heart mother-daughter talk when she got home. I still hadn't told her about Jayden, and while I didn't think she could help me, at least she'd understand how upset I was.

I had just filled up the teakettle and put our special mugs on the table when my phone rang. Mom's name flashed across the screen.

"Hello?" I asked.

"Brooklyn, honey! I'm so glad I got ahold of you. Are you home?"

"Yep, I was making some tea—" I said, but she cut me off.

"Okay, good. I'm so sorry but I forgot to tell you that I wouldn't be home tonight for dinner. Marjorie planned a team mom dinner, and we're going over stuff for senior night. It's still far away, but it's going to creep up on us before we know it. Anyway, do you think you could find something in the fridge to make?"

She went on, but I didn't hear anything she said. I couldn't hear anything she said, because my heart was too busy crumbling apart. A team mom dinner. For Tanner. Right when I needed Mom the most, she wasn't here.

"So you'll be okay?" she asked.

"Yeah, sure, I'm good," I told her, and the worst part

was that she didn't even hear the tears in my voice.

"Great. Love you, sweetie. Call me if you need anything."

She hung up, and I pushed the phone across the counter.

"Don't cry," I told myself, but it didn't work. I couldn't stop the tears; as soon as I blinked, they fell out, one after another.

This was so unfair. Mom was supposed to be here for me. Not for some stupid football thing for Tanner. I was the one who needed her, but she was too busy to realize her real daughter needed her real mom more than anything. It was times like this that brought back all the memories of my horrible, awful recital.

The one Mom never saw.

I hated thinking about it, but this afternoon seemed like the perfect time to feel sorry for myself.

Mom had never dated anyone before she met Stephen. Dad got sick and passed away when I was too young to remember, so it was always the two of us. Everything became different when she met Stephen. Not necessarily bad different, but she was spending tons of time with him, and I missed her. I missed what the two of us had together. I'd wanted a way to get her attention, so I begged my ballet teacher to let me do Clara's dance from *The Nutcracker*.

The one Mom and I had loved when we went away on our girls' weekend. The one she had told me she could see me dancing. The way I figured it was that if I performed it at the recital, she'd remember how much fun we'd had during that weekend and maybe she'd want to spend more time with me again. It was silly, but I had missed her so much at the time that I was willing to do anything to get her attention again.

I'd worked nonstop on the dance. I practiced until I could do it in my sleep, and then I practiced some more. I wanted to be the best. I wanted to wow Mom and make her proud of me.

I wanted her to notice me.

My recital came, and I was ready. I'd spent the week before as I fell asleep imagining what this night would look like. I pictured myself dancing better than I ever had, the audience's applause nearly deafening, and most of all, I envisioned finding Mom in the crowd. She'd be beaming with pride, stunned by the beauty of my dance. She'd remember how incredible I was, and she'd come running backstage to tell me that.

The problem was, that never happened. About ten minutes before my dance, I received a text from her. She was on her way with Stephen, but they were stuck in traffic. There had been some sort of accident on the highway, and all of the cars were at a standstill. She told me she'd do whatever she could to make it, but it didn't seem as if anyone was going anywhere any time soon.

I was devastated. I'd thought about nothing but the recital nonstop for weeks and how it might make Mom notice me, and now she wasn't even going to make it.

I was a mess, but I went out and danced anyway, because what else could I do?

I couldn't focus. As the music began, I thought about the way this night was supposed to have gone and how it had turned out instead. I tried to shake the thoughts. I tried to get my mind right so I could dance, but it was impossible. Everything was scrambled in my head, and when I did a leap, I landed wrong. My ankle twisted, my muscles revolted, and I crashed to the ground. I told myself to get up, to try to keep dancing, but the pain was too much, both from my injury and from what Mom had done. So instead, I collapsed in a heap and remained there as the music to my song continued to play around me. Miss Gretchen rushed onstage to help me. A mother of another dancer, who was a doctor, came backstage to check out my ankle. But none of them were who I wanted to see. I wanted Mom there.

She showed up at the theater about twenty minutes later. I was backstage on a chair with a bag of ice on my ankle. She apologized over and over again, and while she couldn't have helped what happened, it still didn't make things better.

The memory of that night hurt as much now as it had when it happened. I still remembered the weight of the phone in my hand as I read her text. The way my makeup smeared against my fingers when I wiped the tears away. The pain in my ankle when I fell, and the ache in my heart that cut even deeper.

But even if I wanted to forget that night, my injury made it impossible to. Mom took me to the hospital, and we found out I'd badly sprained my ankle. I had to wear a brace for almost a month and then do physical therapy twice a week after that. I never danced again at my studio in Oregon.

It wasn't until we came to Texas that I got the courage to dance again. I *needed* to dance again, because it was the only thing that was the same for me after moving away from my entire life.

But there was a big difference between dancing with a class, with a partner, or on FaceTime with your friend, and dancing a solo by yourself. And I was secretly scared that I'd never be able to dance a solo anywhere again; not after what happened. I never want to feel the way I did onstage that night: ignored and forgotten. Fear has a way of stopping you dead in your tracks, and it pretty much had a super grip on me.

Tonight brought those fears up all over again. Because just like Mom hadn't been there for me at my dance recital, she wasn't here for me now, and I really needed her support.

Chapter 16

Mom was in the kitchen when I got downstairs Monday morning, which should have been a good thing; she had been busy working in the yard with Stephen all weekend, and now we could talk, but it made me more depressed.

"Morning, honey," she said and smiled as if everything was normal. Which, I guess she thought everything was normal since she hadn't been around for me to tell her otherwise.

I gave her a halfhearted smile and popped a piece of wheat bread into the toaster. I missed the breakfasts Mom and I used to have. Once a month, she'd surprised me and made blueberry pancakes. I never knew when they were coming, and there was nothing better than waking up and finding Mom cooking a big stack. On those mornings, she'd take me to school instead of having me ride the bus so that we could take things a little slower and "enjoy our time together," as she used to say. Those were the best mornings ever, and I wished we still did them.

"Honey, I checked with Elliana's mom, and she's going

to take you home from practice today," Mom told me. "I volunteered to bring dessert for the team dinner this week, so I need to go to the grocery store after work. I'll probably be back around the same time you will."

"Okay," I mumbled. "Although it doesn't matter much anymore."

"What?" Mom asked.

"Dance classes. My shot at getting noticed by anyone in the All-City Showcase is ruined. Jayden broke his leg," I say and wait for her sympathy. Maybe she wasn't here yesterday when I needed her, but she was here now.

"Oh, honey, is he okay?" She asked.

I wanted to tell her that I was the one who wasn't okay. But instead, I pushed the words deep down inside of me and nodded.

"That's awful," she said. "Will it be better for the Showcase?"

"No, and that's the problem. I don't have another partner to dance with."

"But you have your solo," Mom said. "You can dance that, and the judges will love you."

"How do you know?" I asked, because Mom had never even seen the dance.

"Because you're incredible. Whether you dance with a partner or by yourself, you're going to impress the judges.

And if it doesn't work out, you still have the studio and Leighton High School."

My stomach did a little dip at the idea of going to Leighton High School. TSOTA was where I wanted to go; I couldn't picture myself anywhere else.

But what choice did I have? Right now, none. I didn't have a dance partner, and I wasn't going to dance alone, which left me with no other options. That meant maybe my fears about going to Leighton weren't so far out there.

Chapter 17

When Elliana and Adeline dropped Jayden off in math class, I did a double take. Jayden had so many signatures on his cast that you could hardly see the bright green color anymore.

"It's too bad you don't have any friends to sign your cast," I joked.

"Right?" Jayden asked. "I told my mom that I might need to break my other leg to make some more room. Pretty much the entire high school football team signed it yesterday when we went to pick up Malik. I bet after this thing comes off, I could sell it and make some good money off of their signatures."

"You could probably make millions alone from Tanner's signature," I said and resisted the urge to roll my eyes at the fact that there probably was someone in this town nuts enough to want to pay for something like that.

"That's the plan. I'm pretty sure I'm set for life after this break," Jayden said.

"At least some good came from it," I said softly.

"Aww, Brooklyn, I didn't mean it like that."

"I know you didn't," I quickly said. "And I do have some good news. My mom said you could come over this Saturday afternoon. I even got her to agree to pizza, so if you're feeling up to it, we could have a movie marathon. Maybe even start a weekly thing until you can dance again. What do you think? I feel like I haven't hung out with you in forever since you're not at dance classes."

"Can we get pineapple and green peppers on the pizza?" Jayden asked.

"On half of the pizza," I said, and scrunched up my nose.

"You've got yourself a deal," Jayden said. "I'd love to come over."

"Great," I said, and it was nice to think about doing something that didn't involve ballet or football. I missed Jayden, and it would be great to spend time with him.

The bell for class rang, and a bunch of the boys from the team barreled through the door at the last minute. They were as loud and obnoxious as usual, and all walked in front of Mr. Jenkins's desk before taking a seat.

"Sorry, Mr. J," Randy said. "Had to grab a breakfast sandwich in the cafeteria."

"Not a problem. You all need your fuel to make it through the day so you can get out onto that field."

"Exactly!" Randy said and followed the rest of the

group to the back of the room, where they sat together. This time I didn't resist the urge to roll my eyes. I rolled them so hard that I'm surprised they didn't get stuck in the back of my head. Because, come on, that was ridiculous. A breakfast sandwich? Fuel? Puh-lease. Mary Rose would go nuts if she found out we were eating stuff like that before rehearsal. She was all about proteins and vegetables. Something told me a greasy sandwich that sat under a heat lamp for an hour and was covered with cheese and bacon wouldn't exactly top her list of foods to eat for energy.

"Okay, let's get started, since we're on a shortened schedule today," Mr. Jenkins said to the class.

"A shortened schedule? For what?" one of my classmates, Callie, asked. Callie was the biggest gossip at our school, and I guaranteed she wasn't too happy to be out of the loop.

"Yep, we have a pep rally," Mr. Jenkins said and gestured to the boys who sat in the back of the room. "These boys have a game this week against Sparson, so the administration thought it would be a great idea to pump them up with a little Leighton Middle School spirit."

"Are you kidding me?" I asked, and everyone turned to look at me. I'd meant to say that in my mind, but the words slipped out. "I mean, I, um, have a lot of work that needs to get done."

I tried to do some damage control, but nothing helped. The class stared at me as if I'd just declared that I was an alien from another planet.

"Can we skip it if we don't want to go?" I asked Mr. Jenkins.

He cleared his throat a few times, as if he didn't know what to say, but he didn't have to, because Randy spoke up for him.

"Why would anyone not want to go to the pep rally? Is there something wrong with you?"

"Why would anyone want to sit in a gym and cheer on a bunch of people who do nothing but run around with a ball and tackle each other? It sounds like there is something wrong with that," I snapped back, the anger I had toward him from the way he acted in the lunchroom still brewing inside of me.

"Oh, like twirling around and leaping across the stage is so much better?" he asked.

"It's a heck of a lot harder," I said.

"Whoa, whoa, whoa," Mr. Jenkins said. "Let's calm down a bit here."

"But she's talking like football isn't important," Randy shot back.

"She isn't saying that—" Mr. Jenkins started, but I cut him off.

"That's exactly what I'm saying," I said, which obviously wasn't the best response. Some of my classmates whispered under their breath and others shifted around in their seats as if I'd committed an awful crime. Jayden stared at me wide-eyed, one girl sat in the corner with her phone out recording everything, and Callie furiously texted on her phone, no doubt making sure she got this news out before anyone else could. Great. Just great.

I sank back into my seat, the fight gone out of me. "Whatever, forget it. I'll go," I said.

"Hold up, let's think about things for a minute. This is an unusual request," Mr. Jenkins said. "But if you really don't want to go, I'm sure we can find a place for you."

"Don't worry, it's okay. I'll go. It's important to show my support for the team. Go, Leighton Middle School!" I said with about as little enthusiasm as I felt. I stuck my hand in the pocket of my hoodie and found my earbuds. I wished I could place them in my ears right now to block out the whispers from all around me. But at least I'd have them for the pep rally. The school might be cheering on the team, but I planned to get lost in the world of *Swan Lake*.

Chapter 18

I survived the pep rally that day, with the help of some very loud classical music, and then found myself going back to the conditioning class, even though I'm not sure why I bothered now that I didn't plan to dance in the All-City Showcase. But I didn't want to let Mary Rose down. I still cared about dancing at the studio, and I was afraid to get blacklisted by her and forced to dance small parts for the rest of my life.

The boys were already in the studio when I arrived. They were seated against the wall, and every single one of them was quietly waiting for class to start.

It was weird.

Very, very weird.

It was as if I were in some parallel universe. Mary Rose clapped her hands together to start class, but she didn't need to. She already had the room's attention.

"What's going on?" I whispered to Logan because the silence was hard to take. It made me uneasy, like when they play scary music in a horror movie and you know something bad is going to happen.

"What do you mean?" he asked.

"You're all acting funny. Like, you're not being obnoxious."

"We're always like this," Logan said, and for him, it was true. He took all of this a little more seriously than most of the boys, but the same didn't hold true for his friends, and I told him exactly that.

"Maybe you are, but Randy isn't."

"It's because of who your brother is. He doesn't want to mess with Tanner's sister."

Unbelievable. I didn't need to be treated any differently from how the boys have always treated me and certainly not because of who my stepbrother was.

"That's ridiculous," I said. "First, Tanner is not my brother. He's my stepbrother. Second, I don't need special treatment. At all."

I went through the rest of class angry and upset. Randy behaved, and as crazy as it sounded, I hated it, because I knew why he was acting this way. He did everything Mary Rose asked of him without one complaint.

When the conditioning class was over and they left the studio, I should've been glad that another class with them was over, but instead, I was numb. Everywhere I looked, I thought about Jayden and how hard the two of us had worked to prepare for the All-City Showcase. And he wasn't gone forever or anything, but it was kind of like a death. The death of my dream to go to TSOTA. And it didn't help that everything in this studio made me think of him.

The door made me remember my first day of class, when the girls had acted all cliquey, but Jayden walked in and announced that he heard there was a new girl and he had dibs on being my partner, because anyone who moved here had to be awesome.

The mirrors reminded me of all the funny faces we'd make at each other during rehearsals. We'd catch each other's eyes in our reflections as we waited for the music to start and try to crack each other up by sticking out our tongues or crossing our eyes.

I thought about the time I'd had a really bad cold and watched the class instead of dancing. Jayden had brought me ginger ale and made a seat out of blankets and pillows, so I was like a bird sitting on a nest.

Or the time we agreed to be partners for the All-City Showcase, and he wrapped me in a giant hug and swung me around and around in the air until I was dizzy, because he was so excited.

I hadn't been here for a long time, but I'd found a true friend in Jayden. I missed my partner, and it wasn't going to be easy to let go of my dream to go to TSOTA.

But that's what I was going to have to do, right?

I didn't have any other choice.

I took a deep breath and pretended to suck in a bunch of courage. I squared my shoulders and headed over to where Mary Rose put away the equipment we'd used today for stretching.

"Do you think we could talk for a minute?" I asked.

"Of course, honey, what's up?" She sat down and patted the spot next to her, which was one of the reasons I loved her. She made sure you always felt important.

"Now that Jayden can't dance with me, I won't be able to be a part of the All-City Showcase anymore."

"Of course you can," Mary Rose said. "You can still dance a solo."

Obviously, she was going to say that. That was everyone's solution. To just dance my solo. And it made sense. Well, if you weren't me. Because here's the thing: For most people, the idea of dancing a solo meant you'd made it, you were good. But I wasn't most people. At least, not after my horrible, awful recital. Now, the thought of dancing a solo and only a solo stopped me dead in my tracks. It made my hands sweat and my stomach twist. I was terrified I'd blow it again, just like I did the last time I danced alone.

"My solo won't wow the judges the way our dance would have. We had those lifts down. They were perfect, and not a lot of people my age can do them. You said it yourself that the potential I showed from those lifts might be enough to get me a spot in the school. There's no way I have time to learn something as good alone."

"I think a solo would be enough. Plenty of people only dance a solo in the Showcase," she said and as I protested, she held up her hand. "But if you have your heart set on also doing a pas de deux, that would help. Your form is incredible when Jayden has you in a lift, and I think the judges need to see that. I might have a solution for you. What if I told you there is someone else at the studio you could partner with? He's good, and I'm pretty sure he'd be able to support you in all the lifts if we start practicing right away."

"There is? Who?" I asked, confused. I knew everyone at the studio, and there wasn't anyone close to Jayden's talent. Boys in dance classes were few and far between, and boys who were as good as Jayden were even harder to find.

"I've been watching the football players during the conditioning classes, and I'm thinking that's the answer to your problem."

"What is?" I asked, skeptical of anything that involved the football team.

"Having one of them learn the routine. Specifically Logan. He's good. He might not have the training, but he's catching on fast, he has the positions down, and if we make the steps a little easier for him, he can probably pull it off and showcase your talent. What do you think?"

What did I think?

Um, that she was crazy.

Certifiably crazy.

There was no way Logan would agree to her idea. The team wasn't exactly into ballet classes. And how would it look if I came crawling back with my tail between my legs after everything I'd said against football? I'd look like such a fool. And I was not a fool.

"I don't know," I said. "I doubt Logan wants anything to do with ballet if it's not connected to football."

"You never know unless you ask," Mary Rose said. "I can see that he's trying to do well. I have a feeling something is motivating him to do better, so that's the key. Practicing with you would be a mutual thing. It would help his skills on the field. If you sell it to him that way, I bet he'd be willing to help."

"You really think so?" I asked, not believing it for one minute.

"I do. Let the idea settle in your mind, and if it sounds like something you might want to try, talk to him. You could be surprised at his response."

I wanted to say no. I wanted to refuse, but at this point, what did I have to lose?

I didn't have a partner, and if I decided not to dance with him, I'd still be without a partner.

However, if he said yes, then there just might be the chance.

"He won't agree to this," I said out loud to Mary Rose. "He isn't going to want to help me."

"People can surprise you," she said.

But Logan agreeing to be my partner wouldn't be a surprise. It would be a miracle.

Chapter 19

Friday night came and I found myself at the last place I wanted to be.

Another football game.

Leighton High was destroying the opposing team, Mom was in full-out football mode, and the stadium was going wild for their University of Texas–bound star quarterback, Tanner. As if they needed another reason to love him. Going to these games seemed like déjà vu: the same night over and over again, with Tanner scoring touchdown after touchdown.

"I wonder what would happen if we lost a game. Just once. Do you think the world would end?" I asked Mia, as she scanned the crowd and recorded everyone with her phone.

"You stop that talk right now," she scolded. "You'll jinx us."

"I'm just saying, it might add a little excitement to things. Winning gets boring after a while."

"You're impossible," she said and turned her phone on me. "Let's talk about more interesting things. Like are you going to ask Logan to help you with the All-City Showcase?

"I really don't think that's the best option," I told her and made a face.

"I mean, I'm not going to lie. I'd rather you stay at Leighton, but you've heard me tell you that a million times. If your heart is set on leaving me, then I think you absolutely need to ask Logan. And I think you need to let me record it," she said.

"That's never going to happen. No way, no how," I told her.

"Think about the hits we'd get."

"I've given you enough footage for the next hundred years. That camera isn't going to be anywhere near the two of us if I ask him."

"So you're going to do it?" Mia asked.

"I said *if* I ask him. Because what if he says no? I'll be mortified, and then how could I show my face at conditioning class again?"

"He won't," Mia assured me. "He not as bad as you think; he's actually really nice. I have math with him, and when he's away from the rest of the team, he's cool. He's helped me with my problems when I'm stuck, and he's smart."

I thought back to how seriously he always took the class, and what Mia was saying made sense. "I could totally see that," I told her.

"So you are going to ask him?"

I couldn't believe I was agreeing to this, but I threw my hands up in the air as if I surrendered.

"I guess. Maybe? I don't know. Ugh! It's too much to think about. I mean, I'd have to figure out what to say, when to ask him, what to do if he says no."

"How about right now?"

"What?"

"Right now. He's over there, and there's no time like the present. Go talk to him. All you have to do is ask him to be your partner, and if he says no, you can walk away and I'll help you drown your sorrows with anything you want from the concession stand. Either way, you'll have your answer instead of waiting around and wondering what he's going to say."

Mia was right. Logan was a few sections over, with the middle school team. They had their practice jerseys on and studied the game intently. But then, as I watched them, something happened on the field and the stands erupted in cheers. The boys pounded on each other's backs and jumped up and down.

"It's ridiculous how worked up people get about a stupid sport," I muttered, but cheered along with everyone so no one could accuse me of not having school spirit.

"Kind of like all those people who go to watch ballets

and clap at the end of each dance number?" Mia asked with a sneaky look in her eyes.

"That's not the same," I told her.

"Oh yeah, you're right. Didn't the football team say that ballet dancers aren't athletes? I mean, if it isn't a sport—"

"Okay, fine, you're right. Point made."

"Thank you," Mia said with a smug look. "And you know what else I'm right about? Asking Logan to be your partner. He's heading up the bleacher steps right now, and if you go follow him, you won't have to talk to him in front of the team. Go, go, go!" she cheered and sounded like the rest of the fans in the crowd.

And maybe it was the electric atmosphere or that little voice in the back of my mind telling me that maybe Logan would say yes, we'd rehearse together, I'd find out that he is good, we'd rock the All-City Showcase, I'd get into TSOTA, and all would be perfect in the world. Whatever it was, it was enough to encourage me to get up and follow him.

Which is exactly what I found myself doing, as I dodged around people like I was a private eye trailing Logan. He got in line for the concession stand, so I did the same. There were a few people in front of me, which made it impossible to call out to him without getting the attention of everyone around me. Could you imagine how embarrassing that would be if he turned me down? The whole school would be talking about how pathetic I was.

The woman behind the counter gave him a hot dog, and he walked over to the condiment bar. Now was the time to make my move.

"Can I have a bottled water?" I asked the girl taking orders when I got up to the front. I kept my eye on Logan, who seemed to be on a mission to add pretty much every topping there was to his hot dog, which worked to my benefit, since it meant that it kept him there.

"Anything else?" she asked.

"No, just that. And fast," I told her, worried I might miss him. When she eyed me up like I was being super rude, I added, "I don't want to miss the game. I have to get back to my seat."

"Of course," she said, and I hated how once I mentioned football she was understanding.

As soon as I got the water, I headed over to Logan. I took a sip so it seemed as if I was doing something. The problem was, something in the air tickled my nose, and I let out a giant sneeze. The water I'd taken a sip of went down the wrong way and started a major coughing fit that was pretty much impossible to stop.

"Are you okay?" Logan asked.

I held my hand up and waved him away. "I'm fine," I said in between coughing fits. My mouth was burning, my eyes were watering, and I must have looked like a complete idiot.

He tilted his head and studied me. "You sure about that?"

"Yeah, it's all good. It just went down the wrong way," I said and instantly felt like the biggest idiot in the world.

He took a giant bite out of his hot dog. Ketchup and mustard oozed out and barely missed falling on his shoe.

I tried to muster up the courage to ask him about the dance, but the words seemed stuck in my mouth, so instead, the two of us stood there awkwardly.

"Okay, well, I'm going to go back to the team," Logan said and began to inch away.

"Wait!" I yelled way too loud, panicked I was going to miss my chance.

Logan stopped.

"I have a question to ask you, and you'll probably think I'm crazy, because believe me, I'm wondering if I am, but I have to ask," I said in a rush, one word tumbling out after the next. I talked so fast that I wondered if he could understand me.

"Sure, what is it? I like crazy. My dad and I root for the Cleveland Browns."

"The Cleveland who?"

"You don't know who the Browns are? Wow, you really

don't care about football. They're pretty much the worst team in the NFL. They *never* win a game. Everyone makes jokes about them, but my dad is from Cleveland and I grew up watching them."

"Yeah, I'm not really much of a football fan," I admitted. "It's not my thing."

"How do you survive in this town? And your family? They're about as football as it gets."

I gave him a very solemn look and pretended to be all serious. "It's hard, I'll admit it. Very hard, but somehow I'm still standing. In fact, the city is thinking of giving me a special medal for courage."

"How very brave of you," he said.

"Right? Luckily, there's ballet. And that keeps me going."

"You really do love ballet, don't you?" he asked.

"More than anything," I said. "But that's the problem."

"How is that a problem?"

"Because my biggest dream in the world has been destroyed. I planned to go to Texas School of the Arts for high school. I've been practicing my Showcase piece with Jayden for weeks now."

"And Jayden broke his leg," Logan said.

"Yep, it's pretty much the worst ever."

"I've seen him all over school on his crutches. It's a tough break."

"Literally," I said, even though there was nothing funny about it. "He's not going to be able to dance with me at the All-City Showcase, and my chances of getting into that school are pretty much gone. That's why I wanted to talk to you. You might be able to help."

"How could I help?" he asked.

"Well, according to Mary Rose, she thinks you can do a lot."

I chewed on my bottom lip and shifted my weight from foot to foot. I wanted to ask him my question. I *needed* to ask him my question. But I was too darn nervous. *Go ahead. What do you have to lose?* a little voice inside of my head reminded me, so I pushed forward.

"Now that Jayden isn't able to dance, I need a partner. And Mary Rose said you're good for someone who doesn't have any formal training. She thinks you could learn the dance I was supposed to do with Jayden. I know you're busy with football, but she promised to help us, and it would only take a little time each week. And it wouldn't be just for me. It would help you with football, because you'll get more one-on-one help and you can use those skills on the field." I was at it again, my big mouth dumping all the words at once, and it felt as if I wasn't just trying to convince him to be my partner, but I was trying to convince myself that he'd make a great partner.

He didn't answer right away. In fact, he said nothing for what seemed like a thousand minutes.

"Forget I asked," I told him, because it was a stupid idea. He obviously didn't want to do it, and I couldn't force him to.

"Okay," he told me.

"Yeah, it was stupid to ask."

"No, I mean okay, I'll help you. I'll learn the routine so you can dance with a partner."

"You will?" I asked, and it was seriously as if I'd fallen into the rabbit hole like Alice in Wonderland.

"Sure. At first I thought ballet was a crazy idea and pretty much had to be dragged there, but it's helping. Coach Konarski has noticed it too, which is exactly what I need to happen. Coach Trentanelli always picks a few eighth graders to start training with his high school team in the off-season. I have to be one of those players. So yeah, sure, I'd love to work with you and use it to help me land one of those spots in the off-season."

"You'll really be my partner?" I asked, still not quite believing this was true.

"Yep, but on one condition."

"Sure, anything," I said, still stunned at how easy this had been.

"Well, you've made it clear that you don't like football.

At all. And I can tell by the way you look at us that you don't like the team."

"It's not that—" I started to try to make things better, but he cut me off.

"It's okay. I figure it's because you don't have true Texas blood."

"True Texas blood?"

"Yeah, football flows through us from the day we are born. You can't help that you didn't get the privilege of living in our great state your whole life. It's actually a bit tragic, if you think about it."

"I'd hardly call it tragic," I said as I thought about all the people who walked around in cowboy boots and blasted country radio in their cars. If that was Texas blood, no thank you.

"Don't worry. I can help you. In fact, it's my duty as a Texan to help you. So the deal is, I'll be your dance partner if you promise to give football a chance."

"Give it a chance?" I asked, confused.

"Yep. All you have to do is let me show you that the sport isn't that bad. Teach you a little bit about the game and what it's all about. I'm not asking you to fall in love with the game, but to respect it and the hard work we put in."

Respect football? A sport where everyone chased a ball

around and tackled each other? That was about as far off as my piloting my own rocket ship to Mars or discovering ancient dinosaur bones in Mom's flower garden.

"Yeah, I don't think that's going to happen," I told him.

"You don't even want to give it a try?"

"What is there to try? Football just isn't my thing."

"Well, it looks like getting into Texas School of the Arts is going to be impossible too, because that's my offer. Take it or leave it."

And I wanted to leave it. Oh, how I wanted to leave it.

"It's never going to happen," I told him.

"That's for me to figure out. Let's give it a shot. If I can't make you see that football actually involves some strategy, planning, and discipline by the time the Showcase happens, we'll call it even. All I ask is that you give football an open mind and a chance."

"You're crazy, do you know that?"

"Maybe, but if I have a shot at making the one person in this whole entire town who doesn't like football change her mind, I have to try, right? It's my Texan duty."

"And if there's a chance that you can learn Jayden's dance well enough that I have a shot at getting into Texas School of the Arts, I have to try, right? It's my ballerina duty."

Logan grinned. "Sounds like it."

I grudgingly stuck my hand out. "Okay, you have a deal. Here's to giving things a try."

He grabbed it, and we shook.

"We'll make a football fan out of you yet," he said.

"And I'll be seeing you Sunday afternoon for our first dance rehearsal."

At that moment, the crowd went wild with cheers and whoops and hollers. Realistically, it was probably because my brother had done some awesome amazing play on the field again, but in my mind, I told myself it was because I was back in the game again. If Logan could pull off what Mary Rose thought he could, maybe I would still have a chance at getting into TSOTA, and nothing could ruin how excited I felt about that possibility.

Not even football.

Chapter 20

As Mom drove me to the studio for my first practice with Logan, my stomach twisted and turned. What if Logan hated ballet? What if he wasn't any good? What if he decided that he didn't want to dance with me? My future was on the line, and if you wanted to get real, it depended on him.

Logan was already at the studio when I got there.

"You showed up," I said, somewhat surprised. I'm not going to lie and say I hadn't worried that he'd changed his mind pretty much every single moment after we talked. But here he was even before I arrived, ready to practice with me.

"I told you I would, didn't I?"

"Yeah, but I didn't actually believe it. I haven't had the best luck these days."

"Relax, I'm here. I can't promise you that I'm going to be any good, but I'll try."

"Thanks," I told him and wished there was a way to truly show him how thankful I was. If we could pull this off, then I might stand a chance of getting noticed by TSOTA scouts, and there would be nothing better than that.

He gestured toward the entrance. "I guess we should go inside, right? I'm pretty sure I'm going to need a lot of practice."

"You have nothing to worry about," I told him, but wondered if that was true.

The two of us went through the door and he headed toward the boys' dressing room. He held up the bag in his hand. "I got some special ballet clothes. I'll be right back."

The idea that he'd gotten clothes for our rehearsal made me hopeful, although the funny thing was that I'd worn leggings and a T-shirt to rehearse today because I didn't want Logan to feel out of place if I had my usual leotard on. I changed and headed into the studio, where I found Mary Rose already there.

"I'm so glad you're giving this a chance," she said. "We're going to make this happen, okay?"

"You think?" I asked.

"I know." She winked at me. "You've got this. You'll be heading to TSOTA next year."

"I hope so," I said. Her words gave me a little extra push of confidence that maybe we could pull this off.

"Well, I'm here to dance, but I'm not quite sure my clothes are," a voice said behind us.

We turned to see Logan in pants that looked as if they

were ready for a flood. The bottoms were more like capris and the top of them dug into his stomach.

"Where exactly did you get your outfit from? Your little brother?" I asked and fought back a laugh. He looked ridiculous.

"I watched some videos online and saw all the male dancers in tight pants. I had no idea where to get some like that, so I figured I'd buy a pair of sweatpants two sizes smaller and they'd fit the same."

"They're definitely tighter," I said. "And shorter."

"I'm kind of afraid that if I bend over, I'll split the back of them," he confessed.

"Yep, let's not do any bending," I agreed. Logan meant well, but he looked so ridiculous in those short pants. A tiny giggle escaped and then another and soon the two of us were laughing so hard that I had tears coming out of my eyes.

"You don't have to wear those," Mary Rose told him. "Dance in whatever you're the most comfortable in. That's when you do your best."

"You mean I can wear my football uniform and helmet?" Logan asked, making me laugh all over again. Maybe Mia was right. Maybe Logan wasn't so bad after all.

"The helmet might not be the best idea," Mary Rose said. "But wear what you've been wearing to the conditioning classes. That's fine for now."

"She's right," I told him. "Change into the clothes you had on when you got here."

Logan looked relieved and went to switch outfits.

Mary Rose nodded at him when he came back out. "Much better. I'm sure you'll find it's easier to dance in that."

"Anything is easier than those other pants. I would've lived in fear of them splitting down the middle the entire time," he said.

"A wise decision," Mary Rose agreed. "Okay, you already know how to do some of the basic positions because of the conditioning class, so today I want to work on how to make them look good. Once you're able to do that, we'll put different ones together in a way that's not too hard for you but enough to make it look like you're dancing as you support Brooklyn and make her look amazing at the Showcase."

"If you think you can do it, I'm game."

"It's all about your extensions, stretching your limbs out as much as you can while making it look seamless," she said.

"Huh?" Logan asked, and I couldn't help but speak up. He looked clueless.

"She means reaching your legs and arms out as far as you can when dancing. Like when you're reaching out to catch the football." I couldn't believe that I was using a football simile, but a girl's gotta do what a girl's gotta do, right?

"Oh, like this?" Logan said and stretched his hands up in the air, but he looked more like he was reaching for something on the shelf than doing a ballet move.

"Yeah, kind of." I turned to Mary Rose for help.

She stepped in front of us. "How about we go through the foot positions first?"

She walked Logan through first, second, third, fourth, and fifth positions. He did okay with each of them, until she added his arms, too. Then Logan became a tangle of limbs, everything going different ways. We had him follow us multiple times, but he continued to mess up.

Mary Rose patiently worked with Logan, but he didn't get any better. In fact, it seemed like he got more and more clumsy as he rehearsed.

I stepped away from the two of them and watched. The way Logan continued to mess up made me think about a girl named Becca at my old studio in Oregon. She was an amazing dancer, but also one of the snobbiest people I knew. She'd watch the rest of the girls dance in our class and wrinkle her nose and make comments about how bad they were. I wondered if she talked about me when I wasn't around. She used to say that you couldn't make a person a dancer; you were either born with talent or not. I always thought that was such a mean thing to say, but I was beginning to wonder if it was true with Logan.

Logan finally reached his breaking point after trying multiple times to do a turn Mary Rose was showing him.

"This is impossble!" Logan said and threw his hands up in the air out of frustration. "It's like rubbing your belly and patting your head at the same time."

"You're doing great; this stuff is hard to get the hang of," Mary Rose said, but it really wasn't. It was a basic combination she used with the younger kids. Maybe Logan wasn't as good as Mary Rose thought. Maybe he really couldn't do this stuff. I didn't even want to think about trying to do the lifts. If Logan couldn't get these steps down, what would happen when he had to pick me up?

I pictured myself crashing to the ground, just like all my hopes and dreams of getting into TSOTA.

Chapter 21

Mary Rose sent Logan off with a bunch of encouraging words, but I wasn't sure anything would help him. And it made me question all the times that she told me I was doing well too. Was she telling the truth? Because I honestly couldn't believe that Logan would figure this out, and she sure made him think he would.

Usually, after rehearsing with Jayden, I'd put my legs up against the wall to let them drain as a way to cool down. However, today I didn't need to because I hadn't done much dancing. Instead, I pulled on a baggy hooded sweatshirt and grabbed my stuff and went out to wait for Tanner, who was my ride home today.

He pulled up in his practice jersey and had one of those thick, disgusting-looking protein shakes. He was always drinking those things and then leaving the water bottles and glasses lying around, the powder clinging to the sides and creating a nasty film on the glasses.

"How was class today?" Tanner asked and took a giant gulp of his drink and then let out a burp.

"You are so gross," I told him.

"I learned it from you," he said, and I seriously felt as if I were arguing with a little kid. He nudged me in the shoulder. "So how was class?"

"Good," I said and tried not to think about how not-good Logan had been. "What about you?"

"Great. Coach ran us through a bunch of drills for the game this weekend, and I think we're in good shape."

"You'll be fine. You guys always win," I said, not to be nice, but because it was the truth. "Jayden told me that Malik was talking to some recruiters too. I'm pretty sure with guys like the two of you on the team, you're the school to beat."

"I hope so. Speaking of Jayden, he was at practice the other day with his mom. You didn't mention that he broke his leg. Isn't he your partner for that dance thing you have?"

"The All-City Showcase," I said, surprised he knew anything about it. "And he *was* my dance partner," I said. "He's not anymore."

To his credit, Tanner looked like he felt bad for me. "Yeah, his leg looked pretty messed up. What are you going to do now?"

If Tanner would have asked me this yesterday, I would've been excited to tell him about Logan and how Mary Rose thought he'd be the perfect solution and how this all still might work despite what happened to Jayden. But that was yesterday. Before I had my first rehearsal with Logan. Now I didn't know what to say, because I honestly had no idea if this would work out after having seen Logan dance.

"One of the guys on the team is helping me," I finally said.

"What team?" Tanner asked, confused, and I didn't blame him. It wasn't like football and ballet went hand in hand.

"The middle school team. Logan Brewer. My dance teacher thought he'd be able to pull the moves off, and it also gives Logan some extra practice, so he agreed to it. He mentioned wanting the extra practice to help get Coach Trentanelli's attention when he picks eighth graders to work with in the off-season." I left out the part about our deal about him turning me into a football fan. I figured that was info Tanner didn't need to know, especially when there was no way in the world it would happen.

"I get wanting to be picked to train with the team— that's huge—but do you think his dancing with you is a good idea?" Tanner asked.

"Why wouldn't it be?"

"He should be focused on football. That's where he's going to learn the skills and drills that he needs to be a good player. Football should always be his first priority. After all, the middle school team is the future of the high school team."

"Are you kidding me?" I asked. "There's a lot he can learn with ballet to become a better player. And what about *my* future? This Showcase is huge to me. There are going to be talent scouts from all over."

"I just wonder if this is good for Logan. Next year he's going to be moving to the high school, and it's a whole different game playing for Leighton High."

Tanner was unbelievable. He continued to argue against Logan helping me with the Showcase. Forget about my surprise over Tanner paying attention to anything important to me. I take that back. I take all of it back. It was better when he was clueless.

Chapter 22

Breakfast during the week was the complete opposite of our weekend family breakfasts. Once Monday hit, it was everyone for themselves. I'd wolf down a bowl of cereal while I listened for the bus to rumble past outside, Tanner would make his disgusting protein shake, while Mom and Stephen usually guzzled down mugs full of coffee and grabbed bagels to be eaten on the run. This had been our routine for the last few months, which is why I was confused when I walked downstairs Monday morning to find everyone around the kitchen table.

Well, everyone but me.

"Did I miss the breakfast meeting invitation?" I asked.

"Sorry, honey. Something came up this morning as we were getting ready for work," Mom said.

"Please don't tell me that Tanner got another scholarship," I said in a voice that made it seem as if I were joking, but secretly I prayed that wasn't what was going on.

"Kind of the opposite," Tanner said.

"That's enough," Stephen shot back.

"So what are we talking about?" I asked as I helped myself to a glass of orange juice from the carton sitting on the table. When no one answered, I felt as if I'd crashed a party where I wasn't wanted.

"More like what are we arguing about," Tanner said, which earned him another look from Stephen. Tanner turned toward me. "I was telling them about how I'm unsure of whether I'm going to take the athletic scholarship now at UT."

"You don't want to go there?" I asked.

"No, I want to go there. I found out I was also accepted early admission to their premed program. I'm not sure I want to play football."

"Not play football?" I asked. Tanner was all about football; there was no way he wouldn't want to play. It was like me and ballet. I'd never give that up.

He ran his hand through his hair so it was all messy. "The premed program is intense. I don't know if I'll have time to keep up with studying if I'm on the team."

"Football is your life," I said.

"I love football, but I don't plan to play it forever. It's not like I'm heading to the NFL after college."

"So you're going to give up a scholarship?" I asked. Inside I was boiling. He better be joking, because I'd had to leave my friends and dance studio and life so he could keep playing football. There was no way I was okay with him simply walking away from it. "That's nuts," I said instead.

"Exactly," Mom chimed in. "You'd be crazy to throw away a full ride to college."

"He's not going to throw anything away," Stephen said. "Tanner will play football at UT."

"Um, I think that's my choice," Tanner shot back.

"Not when you're living under my roof," Stephen said.

For once, I agreed with Mom and Stephen. This was ridiculous. We'd all given up so much so Tanner could play. How could he be so unfair and selfish?

I was about to tell Tanner how mad I was when I saw a flash of yellow out the front window.

"Great!" I yelled and threw my hands up in the air. "I missed the bus because I was stuck in the middle of all your arguing. Now I'm going to be late for school."

"I'll take you," Tanner said. "I already missed lifting this morning, so it's no big deal."

"That's okay," I said, not wanting anything to do with that traitor. "I'll get a ride with Mom or Stephen."

"Your school is in the opposite direction for both of us," Mom said. "It'll be easier if Tanner takes you."

"Yep, no problem," Tanner said. "Let me go grab my stuff and we'll meet back down here in ten minutes."

"Thank you," Stephen said. "But this doesn't mean we're done discussing your scholarship."

Tanner didn't bother to respond. Instead, he got up from the table and headed upstairs.

"Really? Can't you see what he's doing?" I asked. "All he wants is an excuse to get out of our conversation."

I scowled in Tanner's direction. Great. Just great. Because Tanner may have gotten out of the conversation, but now I was the one who was going to be stuck—in the passenger seat of his truck.

Chapter 23

Can you believe the two of them?" Tanner asked me as we pulled out of the driveway. He took his fist and banged it into the steering wheel. He hit it so hard the horn went off. "They're being totally unfair!"

What's unfair? The fact that I'm stuck listening to your whine? I thought to myself. I listened as he went on and on about how Stephen and Mom weren't taking into consideration anything that was important to him. I didn't respond, but believe me, I was seething inside.

I thought about Mom and the researcher job she loved back home. She had cried on the last day of work and still mentioned from time to time how much fun the staff was at her office.

I thought about all of my friends and how they'd thrown a big good-bye party for me at the studio when I left. I still missed them like crazy: the ice cream runs we'd go on in between classes, the giant sleepovers we'd have after recitals, and the days where we spent hours in the studio dancing, simply because that's what we loved to do.

I thought about our little two-bedroom house that I

grew up in. It was tiny, but Mom filled it with pictures of us, blankets Grandma had knitted, and tulips that came up each spring. It was my home.

I thought about all of these things and got more and more mad as I listened to Tanner. My anger bubbled up like a can of soda when you shake it. Finally, I couldn't take it anymore and exploded.

"Maybe you're the one being unfair!"

Tanner paused and actually shut his mouth for a moment.

"What are you talking about?" he asked and seemed genuinely confused.

"You're complaining about how your dad and my mom are reacting to your news, but have you thought about why? Have you even given any thought to what everyone else has done for you? What we have given up? Mom and I moved here for you. For you! We gave up our entire lives because of your football. That was more important than anything else in the world. Excuse me for not agreeing with you about how you don't like my mom and your dad's reactions. Because the reality is, we all deserve to be upset at you."

Tanner pulled up to the light in front of my school, and I practically had my hand on the door before he even stopped. Why wait for Tanner to turn into the parking lot? That simply meant I'd have to listen to him complain more, and believe me, I was perfectly fine walking the extra distance if it meant I didn't have to do that.

"Thanks for the ride," I said as I closed the door. Maybe it wasn't the best way to say good-bye, but I didn't care. I was done with Tanner. There was no way he'd ever get me to see his point of view.

Chapter 24

I'm pretty sure that if I were a cartoon, you'd have seen smoke coming out of my ears all day long. I was furious at Tanner, and there was no way I was going to calm down anytime soon. And the worst of it was, I didn't have anyone to talk to. While Jayden and I had started hanging out after school, watching movies or playing board games, he wasn't the type of friend I'd confide in about something like this. Dasha's mom didn't let her have her cell phone during the school day, and Mia was on a field trip with the Art Club. Talk about the worst possible time to need one of your best friends and not have them.

That's why I had to schedule one of Mia's and my emergency taco heart-to-hearts.

CAN YOU MEET FOR BURRITOS? EMERGENCY!
I texted her.

OF COURSE! WHAT TIME?

**AFTER DANCE CLASS. 6:30 @ LOCOS TACOS
!!!!**

That's all that Mia needed to let me know she was there for me, which is why she's such a good friend. Not that it's very hard to convince each other to go to Locos Tacos; they have the best food ever. I bet you could travel all over the world and eat in thousands of fancy restaurants and never find a meal as good as Locos Tacos. Seriously, if I had to choose between never having chocolate again in my life or their burritos, I'd always pick Locos Tacos hands down.

You'd think that a small silver Airstream trailer with two tiny windows wouldn't be able to make the world's best burritos, but you'd be wrong. There was nothing fancy about the chalkboard sign where they wrote the specials of the day and the picnic tables, which were so old you had to be careful you didn't get a splinter, but when you bit into one of their burritos, with the perfect mix of pulled pork, black beans, cheese, salsa, their top secret hot sauce, and guacamole, you might believe you were eating the best meal on Earth. Which was why Mia and I loved it so much. It was halfway between her house and mine, and because I could cut through the park to get there instead of going on a busy street, Mom let me go whenever I got the craving. It's the perfect spot for an emergency heart-to-heart, and this afternoon was definitely one of those times when I needed to go.

There was a long line when I rode my bike up, but Mia had worked her magic and gotten one of the five tables. She already had food and peach fizzers waiting for us. Peach fizzers were their specialty: a tiny bit of peach juice in sparkling water.

She pushed one of the drinks my way along with a square cardboard tray wrapped in foil. "Here you go: one pulled pork burrito."

I took a giant sip of the peach fizzer and bubbles popped all over in my mouth. I told myself not to drink it all at once, which was pretty much impossible because it was simply that good. Mia and I usually sucked our first ones down and then went back for a second.

"I dream about these things," I told Mia as I unwrapped my burrito.

"They are pretty amazing," she said and pulled out her phone and pointed it at me. "So tell us, Brooklyn, the world wants to know, how much do you love that burrito?"

I took a giant bite and a bunch of the insides came out the other end. I held up my pointer finger to signal to Mia to wait while I chewed, and then when I was done gave her a giant smile.

"Well, Mia, let's just say that if my house was burning down and I had the choice of saving either my most prized possessions or one of these burritos, I'd have a hard time deciding."

"You're nuts," Mia said but laughed.

"Nuts about these burritos," I said.

Mia shook her head and put the phone down so she could pick up her own burrito.

The two of us made our way happily through our burritos for the next couple of minutes. When my stomach was satisfied, I took a break and wiped my messy hands with a napkin.

"So about this meeting. Things are a bit tense at my house . . . ," I started.

"What's wrong? Is Tanner leaving his stinky practice jerseys around again?"

"I wish it were that simple. He surprised us all with some news. He doesn't think he's going to play football in college."

"He's going to try to go straight to the NFL?" Mia asked. "He's good, but I didn't think that was an option."

"No, it's the opposite. He doesn't want to play at all. He wants to focus on his premed courses. He's afraid football will take up too much time."

To Mia's credit, she didn't reply for a moment. And who could blame her? The news was pretty shocking.

"You're joking, right?" Mia asked, and I shook my head. "Why wouldn't he take the scholarship? Tanner not playing football is un-American."

"And unfair. He hasn't even thought about what Mom and I had to leave behind to come here so he could play."

"How about what you gained?" Mia asked, and I could hear that tiny bit of hurt in her voice that she'd been getting more and more lately, especially when I talked about TSOTA.

"There're a lot of great things that happened when I moved here," I said and pointed at her. "You're the number one best thing, but that doesn't mean it wasn't hard to leave the only life I'd ever known. It isn't fair of Tanner to make a decision like this after all we've done for him."

"It does seem crazy; he's so good at the game. The town loves him."

"Wait until they hear about this. It's all anyone is going to talk about, and people aren't going to be happy." Typical, even when Tanner wasn't playing football, he was still the most talked about thing in this town.

"It would make a good story," Mia said, and I could practically see the wheels turning in her mind.

"Nope, no, this is between us. What happens at our burrito heart-to-hearts, stays at our burrito heart-to-hearts."

"Your secret is safe with me," Mia said and pretended to lock her lips and toss the key over her shoulder. "Hey, look on the bright side, at least you won't have to go to football games every week now."

"I didn't even think of that. Maybe there is some good to Tanner not playing football."

"There is," Mia agreed and picked up her drink. "Although, as my best friend, you'll still be expected to come to the games with me."

"So what you're saying is that I'm never going to get away from football?"

"Yep. You're stuck with football and me forever. You should go ahead and mark your Friday nights as busy in your calendar for the next ten years."

As the two of us laughed over burritos and peach fizzers, I thought about how lucky I was to have found a friend like her who could turn things around when life wasn't going my way.

Chapter 25

That Saturday, I finished my morning dance workout with Dasha and headed upstairs, my stomach growling like it always did after a long practice.

But when I walked into the kitchen, I found a silent house that smelled like it always did. A mix of Mom's cinnamon candles and the pine scent of the floor cleaner. This wasn't right. Everyone was supposed to be debating last night's game. The house was supposed to smell like bacon and sausage and maple syrup and coffee. But it was none of those things because Mom and Stephen were still fighting with Tanner. Each side thought they were right, and no one was willing to listen to anyone else. And so this morning the house smelled like our house, which really bummed me out.

I went into the empty kitchen and made myself a gourmet breakfast of strawberry Pop-Tarts and orange juice. I headed to my room, a bit bummed that we were breaking tradition, even if it did mean a pause on the football talk. But that didn't mean I couldn't find something else to do. I propped my computer on my knees and watched videos of the ballet *Giselle*. It's crazy to see all the variations different companies do. I watched a few of my favorites and had just started a new video of the show, one from Italy, when the doorbell rang.

I didn't think anything of it—it was probably one of Tanner's Neanderthal friends stopping by—but then Mom called to me.

"Brooklyn, there's someone here to see you."

Someone to see me? That was odd. Mia usually had art classes on Saturday mornings, but maybe she skipped them this week.

"I'll be right down," I said and paused the video on the computer. I thought about changing for a brief second; after showering, I had put on polka-dot pajama pants and a shirt that was around three sizes too big for me, and my hair was wet and tangled. But why bother? This was Mia, and Mia had seen me tons of times after I'd woken up.

"Why isn't your family at brunch?" I asked as I headed down the stairs. I purposely slid in my socks across the wood floor Mom had just cleaned and into the kitchen, but it wasn't Mia waiting in there.

It was Logan.

I froze, wishing I had taken the time to change my clothes.

Stop being silly, I thought. What did I care how he felt about my outfit? So instead, I struck a pose.

"What do you think? I was trying out costumes for our big dance number."

Logan studied me for a moment. "I think that polka dots would look great on me."

"Perfect! I'll get a pair in your size," I joked. "But I'm guessing you didn't come for the costume. What's up? Did you love our first practice so much that you couldn't wait until the next one?"

"Nope, we're not dancing today," he said with a sneaky glint in his eye. "It's time for my half of the deal. We've got a football game to go and watch."

"Um, what?"

"Football. Remember? I dance with you, you learn all about football? I've come to pick you up for the big game."

I groaned. "You weren't serious about that, were you?"

"Of course I was. And you need to change. Quickly. We have to get moving."

He pulled something out of the backpack he had with him and tossed it at me.

I grabbed the piece of orange cloth and unfolded it. "A football jersey? You have to be kidding me."

"It's a game day essential," Logan said.

"What team is orange and white?" I asked and he

gave me a look as if I had sprouted three heads.

"It's burnt orange, and that's the University of Texas's colors. Haven't you seen it around your house enough now that Tanner is playing for them?"

"I don't really pay that much attention," I told him, and pointed at the shirt. "And I'm not really the type of person to wear a team's shirt."

"Hey, if I'm up for wearing polka dots, you can definitely put on a Longhorns shirt." He pointed at his own Longhorns shirt he had on. "Suit up. We have to get moving or we're going to be late."

"Where are we going?" I asked. My head spun. I wasn't expecting this.

"My house. We watch the game every week. It's low-key and a lot of fun."

"Fun?" I asked and raised my eyebrow.

"Give it a shot," he insisted. "Now really, go change. We need to go, or we'll miss the kickoff."

"Fine, fine, fine," I said and headed upstairs with the shirt to change, wondering what the heck kickoff was and what I'd gotten myself into.

Chapter 26

When Logan had told me that we were watching the game with his family, I'd pictured his mom, his dad, maybe a sibling or two. What I didn't picture was a house jammed full of people and more spilling outside to watch the game on multiple TVs around the house, including a giant one on the patio.

And every single person was in burnt orange and white—University of Texas colors, according to Logan. Some of them were even in it from head to toe with hats, socks, and even a pair of burnt orange pajama pants.

"I guess you were right about wearing this shirt. I would've been the only one not in anything," I told Logan. The shirt was a bit big on me, but I had put it over black leggings and tied a little knot on the side of the shirt to make it fit better. I'd left my hair down for once, deciding against a bun, and put some small yellow star earrings in for a little pop of color. When I sent Mia a picture of myself, she sent back a bunch of thumbs-ups.

"You have to wear burnt orange on game day," he said. "It's the law."

"And apparently, this is the place to watch the game," I told him. "Your house is packed. I thought you said we were watching with your family."

"This is my family. My dad has three siblings, my mom has five, and I have two older sisters with kids of their own."

"And you do this every Saturday?"

"Every Saturday, and usually Sunday, too, for NFL games."

"So colleges play on Saturday and the NFL plays on Sunday?"

He looked at me in amazement. "You really don't know anything about football, do you?"

"Not at all," I admitted. "I mean, I go to Tanner's games, but I don't understand much of what's going on beyond everyone chasing each other around the field and trying to knock one another down. I only stand up and cheer because everyone else does. And unless someone tells me, I never have any idea why they're even cheering."

I figured it was best to leave out the teeny tiny part about listening to music on my headphones, because some stuff is probably better left unsaid.

He shook his head slowly. "You have a lot to learn, which means that I have my work cut out for me. But I like a challenge. We'll make a football expert out of you. Just you wait."

"That's going to be an impossible feat," I said.

"Hey, if you can teach me to dance, then I can figure out how to turn you into someone obsessed with football. Now come on. It's time for your first lesson." He pulled me into the kitchen and right past some of his family members, who looked interested in talking to the two of us.

"This lesson must be important," I told him, after he dodged under the arms of an older lady who tried to hug him.

"It is," Logan said in a solemn voice. "Before we can talk football, I need to teach you about game-day essentials. Specifically, the food. You need to get a fully loaded plate to ensure that you miss as little of the game as possible. You with me on this?"

"Um, I think so," I said as I took a paper plate from him.

"Good. So the secret is to get your drink and silverware first. That way you can tuck them into your pocket and your hands will be free to carry your plate. Because if you do it the other way around, your hands will be full."

"You're a genius," I said. "I'm so glad you've solved such a major world problem. Now I can sleep better at night."

"You may joke about it, but I'm pretty sure you'll thank me later."

The two of us grabbed cans of soda and silverware, but there was a problem.

"Um, your plan didn't include what to do when you have leggings on and no pockets."

Logan looked stumped for a moment, then held up his pointer finger as if an idea suddenly came to him. I could practically see the light bulb pop up over his head. "Easy: Make sure you hang out with someone who has lots of pockets. I've got some on both sides, so we're set."

I gave him my stuff and followed him as we made our way through the food table.

"So what foods should I get for the full experience?" I asked, because I could tell Logan liked to act like an expert on all things football.

He studied the table as if he were making very serious decisions. Finally, he pointed at a Crock-Pot with something orange in it. "That's a must. You need some buffalo chicken dip. Lots of it. It's my aunt's recipe, and she refuses to give us the secret ingredient. She claims that she plans to take it to her grave, which is totally unfair. Believe me, you'll feel the same once you try it."

I put a large serving on my plate along with a bunch of other things Logan pointed out. Some seven-layer taco dip, pulled pork, pizza bites, nachos, and cheesy sauce.

"Okay, and then the last step for the game-day grub is to grab one of those bowls for the chili. You can rest your plate on it."

"Wait, we're going to eat chili, too?" I asked, not sure where I was going to fit all of this. And none of this was what I usually ate as a dancer.

"Chili is the centerpiece of the meal. It's one of the most important foods on college football Saturday," Logan said and dished us both up giant bowlfuls, which he then sprinkled with mounds of cheese. "You can't watch football without it."

I took my bowl, balanced my plate on top of it, and followed him outside, where we sat down at a picnic table near one of the TVs.

"Is this team any good?" I asked after I tried the buffalo chicken dip. Logan was right; that recipe was amazing.

"The Longhorns are always good," Logan said with this look on his face that told me I shouldn't even be asking this question. Like it was something obvious I should've already known. "Although this season they've lost more than they've won, but I'm not giving up hope on my boys."

"Your boys?" I asked. Football was so weird. What about it made fans turn crazy and act like their lives were over if their team didn't win? Why did people gather together every week to watch the games and pledge their undying love to their team? And dressing up in team gear seemed silly to me. I didn't get it, and I was pretty sure I never would.

"They're my boys for life," Logan said and then focused

159

on the TV. He jumped up and began to cheer. Everyone around us did too.

"Go, go, go!" His family yelled to the TV screen. I may be clueless about most things football, but I did know that when someone is holding the ball and heading toward the goalpost, you want them to run like crazy and not get tackled. At least, I think you do? Right?

The player slammed the ball down on the ground and held his hands in the air. Everyone around me went nuts. As in, they were pounding on the tables, hugging each other, and thrusting their fists up in the air. I may be mistaken, but I was pretty sure I even saw an older man with tears in his eyes. These people gave new meaning to the term "die-hard fans."

"So what just happened?" I asked Logan after everyone calmed down.

"Seriously?" Logan asked.

I shrugged. "Like I said, I really don't know anything about the game."

"This is awful. I've been doing it all wrong, haven't I?"

"Doing what wrong?"

"This football thing. Right now you probably think it's nothing but a bunch of crazy fans who get together, stuff their faces, and yell like maniacs at the TV."

"Well, I mean, it's kind of true. . . ."

"That's where you're mistaken, Brooklyn. Football is so much more than that. It's about hard work, discipline, and being a superior athlete. And I'm here to show you that."

I raised my eyebrow at "superior athlete," but I didn't say anything to Logan.

"The first thing I need to do is start at square one and teach you how the game is played. How are you ever going to respect the sport if you can't understand it?"

"You might be right. After all, it's your Texan duty," I said, using the words that he'd said when we first made this deal.

"Exactly," he agreed. And with that, Logan began to tell me every single thing that was going on during the game. He went over every play and actually made the game easy to understand. And the best part was that he didn't make me feel dumb for living in Leighton and not knowing a single thing about the game.

"So you have to memorize certain moves?" I asked.

"Plays," Logan corrected me and then nodded. "It's a huge part of football. It's our plan of action on how to move the ball down the field. But the thing is, we can't use the same play every time, or the other team will know how to stop us. So we memorize tons and tons of different ones and then wait to see which one we're going to use."

"That's a lot of work," I said. "I always thought football

was doing the same thing every time and hoping to get to the end of the field without being tackled."

Logan shook his head. "Not at all. It's tons of practice and memorization. We need to know what we're going to do on the field, since we work together as a team. We learn and prepare for all the different possibilities that might happen. Coach has us running all different kinds of plays that we learn. We also spend a lot of time watching videos and going over them."

What he was saying reminded me of ballet and all the choreography that I had to learn. I'd never thought I'd ever put ballet and football together, but learning the plays seemed a lot like learning a new dance.

"Okay, watch carefully. This is a big play," Logan said and pointed to the screen. "Texas Tech is winning right now, but if we get the ball, we'll be in the lead. All he has to do is run to the end zone and make a touchdown."

I watched as UT got the ball and the player raced down the field.

"Run!" I cheered as he got closer and closer to the end zone. And you know something? Logan was right. Football was a lot more interesting to watch when you knew what was going on.

Chapter 27

fter halftime, Logan turned to me and gestured to the inside of the house.

"Okay, it's time for dessert," he announced and rubbed his stomach.

"Dessert? After all that other stuff?"

"Oh yeah, you haven't finished eating until you've had dessert. Stay here, I'll go get it." He sprinted off before I could protest and returned about five minutes later with two giant bowls, each with a brownie, ice cream, caramel, and a mound of whipped cream.

"Um, you're going to have to roll me out of here if I eat this. I'm pretty sure I might bust," I told him.

"Take a bit. After you try it, you won't have any problems finding room for it in your stomach."

And like everything else today, he was right. It was amazing.

The two of us were making a good dent in our brownies when an older woman came over. She had a little girl in her arms with pigtails that had burnt orange and white ribbons in them.

"Hi, I'm Natalia, Logan's sister, and this is Izzy," she told me and pointed at her daughter. "We've heard all about how good a dancer you are."

"You have?" I asked and turned to Logan. He gave me a sheepish smile and shrugged.

"Izzy here loves ballet," Natalia said and placed Izzy down and pointed at me. "This is Brooklyn, and she's a dancer. She performs on the stage, and your uncle Logan is going to dance with her."

Izzy's eyes grew huge, and I remembered how exciting it was when I was little and met older dancers. But she wasn't the only one who was impressed. I couldn't believe Logan had told his family about us. Truthfully, I'd fully expected him not to say a word about it. It wasn't like ballet was a cool pastime for football players.

I kneeled down so I was on Izzy's level. "Hi, Izzy. Do you dance too?"

She nodded shyly.

"I bet you're great at twirling. Do you want to show me?"

She grinned and held out her arms and began to spin. She went around and around, and when she finally stopped, she lost her balance and fell in a heap of giggles.

"You're great!" I told her. "You looked like a real ballerina."

I didn't think it was possible for her to grin bigger than

she did. Her face shined with happiness, and it was pretty crazy to think it was because of what I said.

"It's nice to be able to meet you," Natalia said. "We're all rooting for you to get into that school."

"Thank you," I told her and waved at Izzy as the two walked away. I turned to Logan. "You told them about us?"

"Sure, I mean, I might have mentioned ballet and helping you with the Showcase."

"Thanks," I told Logan.

"For what?"

"For not hiding ballet and looking at it as if it isn't important like half this town does."

"Believe me, I understand what it's like to really care about something. And you all train and practice just as hard as we do. That's what it's like with football for me. I get it."

"People don't usually get it about ballet."

"It's what you love. That makes sense. And remember, there's also a bonus in there for me, too. If I can get you to respect football, it also means that I'll convert the only person in Leighton who doesn't care about the game, so it's not like I'm losing out on this deal."

"Something like that," I said and made a face at him. I pointed to the screen. "Speaking of football, isn't that player about to score a touchdown?"

Logan instantly focused his attention on the TV. "You're right! See, I did teach you well!"

"You're a great teacher," I said and cheered along with him and the rest of his family, because for once, this crazy game actually made sense.

Chapter 28

I wish I could say that Logan caught on to ballet the way I was able to understand a lot more about football after he had explained it that weekend. Unfortunately, that wasn't the case.

At all.

The next practice was more of the same. Logan tripping over his feet, messing up the steps, and generally making me scared to death that we weren't going to pull this off.

I tried not to get upset, but that's hard to do when your entire future is at stake.

"I don't understand," I finally said after Logan stepped forward instead of to the back and collided into me. "You do all of this so well during conditioning."

"I'm trying, I swear," Logan said, and I felt a flash of guilt at getting on his case when he was helping me. "I have the steps down, but when I put them together, they kind of jumble into a big, confusing mess."

"I'm sorry," I said. "I would probably be the same way if I tried to play football."

"And remember," Mary Rose said to me. "It took you

years and years and years to get this good. We can't expect Logan to be perfect."

But you were the one who suggested he dance with me. That he could take Jayden's place, I wanted to say. I held back my words, though, and we walked through the dance again, marking the steps to help Logan get it down.

"Think of it like your coach going over the plays," Mary Rose told him. "You're good at memorizing plays, and this is similar."

Logan nodded and tried. He tried so hard, we could all see that, but something wasn't clicking. And the more it didn't click, the more frustrated I got, even though I tried not to.

"You're supposed to go left!" I snapped when he ran into me for a third time and stepped on my toe. I threw my hands up in frustration and walked across the room to get away from him.

Logan sank to the ground and looked about as defeated as I did.

Mary Rose stood between the two of us, and her eyes went from Logan to me. I could tell her mind was spinning; she tapped her pointer finger against her other hand like she does when she's trying to work out a piece of choreography.

"How about you take a break for today, Brooklyn?

Logan and I can stay here a little longer, and then we'll get back together again at our next practice. Does that work?"

"Isn't the idea that we dance together?" I asked.

"You will, but I'm thinking that right now Logan might benefit from working one-on-one with me. What do you think?" she asked him, and he nodded right away. "We're not kicking you out because we don't want you here. The two of us will work together on a few things to make sure that Logan has it down so that we're not wasting our time."

"Okay," I said, because what we were doing now obviously wasn't working. And maybe it would help. At least, I hoped it would, because if things stayed the way they were right now, I was in deep trouble and could kiss any hope of getting into TSOTA good-bye.

Chapter 29

I left the studio wishing and hoping that Mary Rose could work some magic. I thought about texting Jayden to tell him my fears. I had been keeping him updated about our progress every time he came over to hang out. Jayden assured me that Logan would catch on, but I wasn't too sure.

I fished around in my bag for my phone to call Jayden and settled onto the bench outside the studio.

It was the perfect type of day outside, and the sun warmed my face. I thought about Oregon weather. Fall would be starting and it would be cold and, truthfully, miserable. It rained a lot there, and while there were a million things I missed, the weather wasn't one of them.

I found my phone, but when I unlocked it, I saw I had 118 messages.

"What the heck?" I said.

That had to be some kind of mistake. I don't think I'd ever gotten that many messages at once in my entire life. Mia texted me a lot, so much that sometimes when I opened my phone, it took a while to read through all of them, but never this many. I'd only been away from my phone for about an hour.

I checked the messages and discovered that they weren't from Mia. In fact, her name wasn't on any on them. Instead, I had messages from a ton of my classmates and numbers I didn't even recognize. People I never even talk to at school, so I had no idea how they'd even gotten my phone number.

"What's going on?" I asked out loud. *Should I open them? Do I want to open them?*

I scrolled through the texts and it only took a few seconds to figure out what that something else was.

They were about a video Mia posted.

A video that everyone was talking about.

Leave it to Mia to post something that gets everyone to her channel again. It's only a matter of time before she gets a job on ESPN. But what did that have to do with me? Why are people talking to me about the video?

I clicked on the link that someone had sent, and I didn't have to watch long to find out my answer.

"Hi, everyone! Good morning! This is Mia Tarvis bringing you the news you want and the news you didn't even know you needed, especially when that news involves Leighton High's football star, Tanner Kratus. Yep, you heard that right. I have breaking news that I couldn't keep to myself."

The image went from Mia to Tanner on the football field. It was last week's game, the one that happened shortly after Tanner heard about his scholarship. The footage showed him on the field as his coaches spoke to the crowd and congratulated him on the University of Texas. The crowd was going nuts for him, even more so with the announcement of the scholarship, if that was possible.

"Last week we celebrated Tanner's offer to play ball at the University of Texas, but this week the party is over. Rumor has it that he still plans to go to UT, but not to play football. I repeat, your favorite Leighton High quarterback is not going to play football."

The video cut to a cartoon crowd looking shocked, which would have been pretty funny if she weren't playing our conversation from Locos Tacos over it.

Our secret conversation that she'd promised not to tell anyone about.

The one the whole world now knew.

The number of views at the bottom of the video was a little over six hundred. Six hundred people had already watched this video, and it was only posted two hours before. I didn't want to look at the comments. You'd have to be an idiot not to know what people in Leighton were going to say about Tanner's news.

Tears welled up in my eyes as I thought about what

Mia had done. I'd told her this in secret. I'd trusted her to keep quiet. That's what friends do. Why would she have shared this information?

I thought back to dinner with her. She'd recorded me eating the burrito, and she must have left her camera on afterward. Had she done it on purpose? On accident? Did it even matter?

The only thing that mattered was the fact that she'd taken the information and shared it with everyone. And for what? To get more views? To bring people to her video page? Was that more important than our friendship?

As if things couldn't get any worse, Mom pulled up right at that moment.

"What are you doing here early?" I asked. Technically, I still had another half hour of practice.

"Get in," Mom said, her voice hard and angry.

I stayed rooted to the spot and pretended I didn't hear her. Maybe if I didn't respond, she wouldn't see me.

"Brooklyn Gartner, get in the car now, or I'll come escort you into the car myself, and it won't be pretty."

Nope. Guess not.

I trudged toward the car. It was only about ten steps, but you better believe that I walked those ten steps as slowly as I could. I climbed into the front seat and wished I could hide my earbuds up my sleeve and tune out the conversation we were no doubt about to have. I guessed telling her about Logan was out right now.

"So, I watched a video today. And it appears that a large part of the community has too," Mom said before she even drove away from the studio. "I thought I should come here early to talk to you about it."

"I'm sorry, Mom. I didn't mean for that to happen," I told her and wished I could show her that was the truth.

"That was private information that only we knew about, Brooklyn. I find it pretty hard to believe that Mia didn't get the information from you."

"I told Mia about Tanner, but that was it. I didn't know she was going to share it with every single person on the Internet. It was supposed to be something between us."

"Then what made her do that?" Mom asked, a little softer this time.

"I have no idea," I said, and it was the truth. Of all the text messages on my phone, none of them were from Mia, and she was the one I most wanted to hear from. As mad as I was at her, I wanted to think that maybe there was a reason. Maybe she had some great story for why she'd taken our family's secrets and made them her news.

"What she did wasn't right," Mom said. "But that doesn't let you off the hook. It wasn't your news to tell. Tanner told us all of that in confidence, and now a lot

174

of people he wasn't ready to talk to know what he's been thinking about. This isn't about you; it affects Tanner's future."

I hadn't even thought about Tanner. What would he think now that I'd told his secret to everyone? He was going to hate me. I groaned and slid down in my seat, wishing I could disappear. In a town like Leighton, you don't walk away from football. And based off of how many views the video had already gotten, the town definitely wasn't about to let that happen.

"I'm sorry," I said. If I had to apologize a million times, I would. But I had no idea how to make this right. And then Mom said the worst thing in the world. The words I never wanted to hear.

"I'm disappointed in you, Brooklyn. I expected better."

And I expected better from Mia, I thought, but I didn't dare say those words out loud. Something told me that now was the time to stay quiet. I only wished that I would have felt that same way when I'd been talking to Mia.

Chapter 30

I told Mom I wasn't feeling well when I got home and was going up to my room.

"That's fine, honey, but you're going to have to face Tanner. You owe him an apology."

As I headed up the steps. I wanted her to follow me. I wanted to talk more about what had happened with Mia and about Tanner's choice in general, but she stayed downstairs.

I crawled into bed and wished I could hide under my sheets for the rest of my life. It would be easier than facing everyone after what I'd done. My phone sat in my dance bag. I hadn't pulled it out since Mom had picked me up, and while I wanted to see what Mia had to say, there was now a side of me that didn't want to check. What if she hadn't even texted me yet? What if she had, and hadn't apologized? My brain spun a million awful scenarios and just made me feel worse.

I heard Tanner and Stephen came home a few hours later, but no one came up to my room. I waited for Mom to check on me, but she never did, and that hurt almost as much as Mia's betrayal.

Chapter 31

I woke up super early the next morning and changed into my leotard. I hadn't slept well, and my body hummed with nervous energy. I couldn't stop thinking about the secret I had told and what Mia had done with it. I needed to dance. I needed to lose myself in the music. It was the only thing that would help.

I crept down the steps and tried to be as quiet as possible. I avoided the creaky spot on the floor in the front hallway and didn't turn on any of the lights. Except when I opened the door to the basement, I discovered that all the lights were on. I tried to remember if I had turned them off the other morning when I had FaceTimed Dasha, but I couldn't be sure.

I turned the corner, and there, working out on the weight bench, was Tanner.

The last person I wanted to see.

My stomach dipped. I wasn't prepared in any way to talk to him yet. I hadn't even talked to Mia to get the whole story. Luckily, he had his headphones on and hadn't noticed me, so I turned around to race out before he saw me.

"Brooklyn, wait," he said.

Shoot. I paused on the steps and tried to decide what to do. Should I head upstairs and pretend I hadn't heard him? Or turn around and face him? I knew what option I wanted to choose, but I had made this mess, and I needed to own up to it. It was the right thing to do. Too bad doing the right thing isn't always so easy.

"Hey," I said hesitantly. I had no idea how he was going to react to things. "I didn't think anyone was down here. It's always empty in the morning."

"Ouch, way to make a guy feel guilty about not working out as much as he should."

"Sorry, I didn't mean it like that," I quickly said. This was going downhill fast.

"Relax, I was joking."

"Oh, okay," I told him, not quite sure what to do. Standing in front of him after what had happened gave me that same nervous flutter I got before a big performance.

"Do you think you could spot me for a few minutes, and then I can leave you to work out here alone?"

"Yeah, sure," I said going over to him as he lay on the bench. I wasn't sure what to make of all of this. He was acting as if everything were normal, but it wasn't. Not at all. And it was my fault. He had to have watched the video, right? I'd gotten all of those text messages, so I couldn't imagine how many he must have gotten. So why hadn't he said something? Was this some kind of weird psychological game where he was trying to mess with my mind? If so, he was doing a pretty good job at it.

I continued to spot him while he lifted, and I went back and forth about whether I should say something. I would open my mouth and then close it again.

Finally, I dove right in. I had to.

"Um, did you see the video that Mia posted?"

Tanner sat up. "You mean the one that has over five thousand views?"

My eyes got wide. "Five thousand views? Mia must be freaking out."

"Is that why you two posted it? Did you tell everyone my secret to get views?" he asked, and he didn't sound mad. It was more like he was sad. And that made me feel a million times worse, if that was even possible.

"I didn't tell her so she could post it," I said, even though that still didn't make things right. "But I did tell her about how you weren't sure you wanted to play football at UT. I told her as a friend, but it wasn't my news to share. And I never in a million years thought she was recording me. If I'd known, I wouldn't have said a word."

Tanner ran his hand through his hair. "It's caused a lot of problems for me. Big problems."

"I'm sorry," I said, because I didn't know what else to say. I had no idea how to make something like this right. "I had no idea this would happen. Mia was my best friend, and I trusted her. She took information I gave her that was secret and shared it with everyone. She told people about your decision when it wasn't her business to tell. Now everyone knows, and it's my fault."

"Sharing my news wasn't cool at all," he said and let out a giant sigh. "But it would have come out eventually, so I guess it was kind of like yanking the Band-Aid off fast."

"That comparison doesn't make me feel better," I said.

Tanner sat up on the weight bench and put his hands on his knees. "This big-decision-making stuff is hard. There's nothing easy about it."

"Tell me about it," I told him, thinking about my solo and finding the courage to believe in myself and dance alone in front of everybody again.

"I love football, don't get me wrong, but it's not going to be my life. People forget that I'm actually a person with other things that matter to me. It's like I've played football so long that people could never imagine that I might have other interests or want to try new things."

"The town thinks they know what's right," I said, understanding exactly what he was saying.

"Mia's video gives them one more reason to talk about

what they think is best for me. But I'm not playing football for them, and I'm not making choices for them."

I thought about the night of the recital, when I danced for Mom. To get her attention. And how for so long dance hadn't been about me, but about what I'd lost and wanted to find. Maybe that wasn't the way it was supposed to be.

"I'm sorry I was so awful that day in the truck when you drove me to school. Believe me, I get that you want to make your own choices and do what makes you happy, but it's hard to understand when I'm the one who had to move here for you and football. I'm so nervous about getting into Texas School of the Arts, and here you are with a full scholarship to the University of Texas and you don't even want to go. It made me upset. It still does, but it's not your fault. I think I'm a little bit jealous."

"Don't be jealous. I'm terrified to step away from football. I keep wondering if I'm making the wrong choice. What if med school isn't for me? What if it's too hard? What if I miss football?"

"But you won't find out until you try, right?" I asked him, and it seemed as if my question was just as much for me as it was for him.

"You've got that right." Tanner stood up. "I better get moving. Thanks for listening."

"Sorry again about everything," I told him.

"We're good. Just promise me that you'll make your decisions for yourself and no one else."

"Promise," I told him. He nodded and headed upstairs, while I was left standing in the basement wondering why that promise seemed so impossible at the moment.

ia finally texted me.

And then texted me again.

And again. And again.

She sent so many texts that I almost missed not hearing from her. She sent so many messages in a row that my phone looked more like a strobe light the way it lit up when a new one came through.

She wouldn't leave me alone now.

She told me that she had taken the video down and deleted it. Her texts were full of apologies. But what's the use? Apologizing wouldn't take back what she'd done, and everyone at school had already seen the video.

Which is why I decided to tell her exactly how I felt in a language she'd understand.

I set my phone up on my desk, propped up on some books, and hit the record button. It was surprisingly easy to talk. Usually, I was awkward about being on camera, but today I was still upset enough not to care.

"Hi, Mia. Since you love to spread news through videos, I thought I'd communicate in the same way. Which is why I'm making this to tell you to stop trying to get in touch with me. You really hurt me, and I don't want to talk to you. I don't want to text you. And I don't want to make any more videos like this. So please leave me alone."

I hit the stop button with such force that my phone fell down and I was afraid I'd cracked the screen.

I picked it up and sent the video to Mia. Maybe it was mean of me, but I have to admit that I felt a little satisfying zing inside. Mia wasn't the only one who could record videos, and all I needed was one view to make sure my message was heard.

Chapter 33

The rest of the school week was the worst ever. I refused to answer any questions that anyone had about Tanner's news and went out of my way to avoid Mia at school. I walked the opposite way when I saw her and ate in the library because I didn't want to talk to her. I wasn't ready to talk to her. What in the world did you say to someone who had revealed one of your biggest secrets?

On Saturday morning, I raced down to the studio for my weekly dance session with Dasha. I needed to fill her in about everything going on, and it would help to talk to someone who wasn't from Leighton.

"Good morning, sunshine!" Dasha said through the screen when I dialed her number, and I wished I could feel as happy as she did.

"Morning," I said, but I wasn't able to muster the same enthusiasm, and Dasha saw right through my fake smile.

"What's wrong? Spill it," she said in that way only a best friend could.

"Everything," I said and told her all about how Tanner didn't think he wanted to play football, the fighting going on in our house because of it, and how Mia had spilled the news. When I was done, she let out a low whistle.

"That's pretty awful," she said, and I instantly felt a little better getting it all off of my chest. "I can't believe Tanner would do that after you and your mom moved there so he could keep playing football."

"That's what I thought when he first told us too. Believe me, I was so mad. And then my way of thinking changed. You're going to think this is nuts, but the more I think about it, the more not playing football in college is kind of brave of him."

"Ditching out on football is brave?"

"I talked with him the other morning and he got me thinking," I told her and tried to explain myself. "Football is his life. It's always been his life, at least that's the way everyone around him saw it. But he's interested in other things too. It's just that no one ever saw that. So if you think about it, it's pretty brave to walk away from something he knows really well, to go after something he doesn't."

"I guess if you put it that way," Dasha said.

"It's cool that he's not letting other people tell him what's best."

"Well, I wish he would have had this realization before you and your mom moved to Texas."

"Believe me, I wish he had too. I miss you so much.

And right now, dancing is still my one true love," I told her, which was true. But talking with Tanner had also made me realize that dancing didn't always have to be my only true love. It was okay to like different things or want to try something new. And maybe one day I would. However, right now, in my basement with Dasha, all I could think about was working on my solo. I needed to get it perfect; I had to impress those judges.

"Let's dance, then," Dasha said, and it was as if she had been reading my mind.

"Sounds like a plan," I agreed. "In fact, let's start with my solo."

"Whoa, who are you, and what's happened to the real Brooklyn?"

"I'm feeling different today. Brave," I told her with a wink. "The All-City Showcase is coming up, so I need to make sure I'm ready."

"You don't have to convince me," Dasha said. "Show me what you've got."

And that's what I did. I danced through my solo three times, and every time I restarted the music and launched into the opening steps, I became stronger and stronger.

"You've got this," Dasha told me. "You're ready."

"You think so?" I asked, and instead of being fearful, I was hopeful.

"I know so. Now, let's go over some of the stuff we learned this week, so when we both go to the Juilliard intensive together, we can amaze the teachers with all of our skills."

And how could I argue with that?

The two of us danced and danced and got lost in a world where nothing else mattered but the music, our movements, and the stories we created through dance. And in those movements, life was perfect. Absolutely perfect.

Chapter 34

Dasha and I were going through our cool-down exercises when the door to the basement opened and Mom called down to me.

"Brooklyn, there's someone here to see you."

Mia.

I froze and gave Dasha a panicked look.

"Are you okay?" she asked, and I shrugged. Because I wasn't. Not if that was Mia at the top of the steps. Trying to call me was one thing, but stopping by my house so I was forced to talk to her was a whole different kind of problem.

"Who is it?" I asked, my voice shaky.

"Logan's upstairs," Mom said. "He says it's important."

I exhaled the giant breath that I had been holding. Thank goodness.

"Dance partner Logan?" Dasha asked.

"Shhhh," I told her. I didn't want Logan to think I was talking to everyone about him. I called up to Mom, "I'll be there in a minute."

"I want to meet him," Dasha said.

"Not today," I told her, because for some reason, I wanted

to keep my two worlds separate. It had been so good to dance with Dasha this morning and forget about everything that was going on here. Introducing her to Logan would cause my worlds to collide, and I wasn't ready for that. Dasha was home. She was safe. She was my escape when things got to be a little too much here. I wanted to keep it that way.

"I'll talk to you later," I told her and gave her a quick wave as she protested. I ended the conversation and felt bad, but you've gotta do what you've gotta do.

I headed upstairs and found Logan in our family room. He stood by the bookcases that were on either side of the TV. One of them was full of pictures of Tanner playing football, and the other was of me in different recitals. It was kind of embarrassing, a shrine to both of us, but Logan seemed superinterested in it.

He held up a picture of me in a hot pink tutu with my hair in a side ponytail. I was maybe in second grade. We'd done a jazz routine to "Girls Just Wanna Have Fun," and our wild costumes showed it.

"That's you, huh?"

"All of these are."

He pointed at my workout clothes. "And you were dancing right now?"

"Yeah, my mom and stepdad made a studio for me in the basement."

"Do you ever not dance?" he asked.

"Hardly," I said.

He studied a few more of the pictures Mom had displayed of me and pointed at my workout gear. "You really love ballet, don't you?"

"Is there something bigger than love? Because that's how I feel."

He picked up a picture of me when I was in *The Nutcracker*. It was my first real performance. I'd felt so important dancing in the same ballet as all of those older girls who held the principal roles. I was only six and played a mouse. The makeup lady had drawn on little whiskers, and after the show was over, I'd refused to let Mom wipe them off. I'd slept with them on and cried when I woke up the next morning and they had smeared. I'd always loved that show. It used to be my favorite. Until it wasn't.

"What about you? Isn't it the same with football?" I asked.

"Yep, there's nothing better than being out on the field. I don't even care about the people in the stands who are watching. It's not about that. It's about me and the game and being able to play."

"You're right," I said, but there was also a little voice in the back of my head reminding me that's not how I always felt. *You wanted to dance for your mom, remember?* And it was true, the dance from *The Nutcracker* hadn't been for me. "I can't imagine anything greater than losing myself in something I love."

"There's nothing better," Logan said.

"Nothing at all," I agreed, and even though we were talking about different things, we weren't. It was the same feelings, the same love that we had, and maybe I had no interest in football and didn't understand the obsession this town had for it, but I got it. I understood why Logan loved it.

"A lot of the guys make fun of the conditioning classes that we're doing, but they've helped me. A lot. Coach even said something to me about how I can turn and pivot faster when I have the ball than any of the other guys on the team."

"That's a good sign, isn't it?" I said, excited for him.

"A very good sign. And right now I can run a forty-yard dash at 5.9 seconds. Coach said that if I'm able to get it down to 5.4, then I'll get picked to do the postseason conditioning with the high schoolers, something only a few middle schoolers are allowed to do."

"That's incredible," I told Logan. "It sounds as if you're doing everything right. And ballet is helping."

He nodded. "It is. I think I can lower my time. The

conditioning classes and our rehearsals are helping my flex-ibility and stride length a ton, which means that if I keep working out with you, I should be able to get even faster."

"I have to admit, I didn't realize so much work went into football," I told him. "I mean, I kind of did, with Tanner, but still."

"That's what I've been trying to show you," Logan said. "And today It's on to the next step of teaching you to respect the game."

"Oh yeah, and what's that?"

"You'll see," Logan said with a grin on his face that made me think he was up to something. "Now go get dressed in something you can move around in outside. We've got to be somewhere."

"Can I shower? I'm a bit grungy." I pointed to my out-fit and my hair, which was in a messy, sweaty bun.

"You're going to get even more dirty where we're going." He laughed.

"I'll be fast," I told him and raced upstairs before he could protest. I thought everyone would thank me if I took a shower after dancing with Dasha, even Logan.

Chapter 35

I showered and changed in record time and met Logan in the kitchen. He was drinking a glass of orange juice and talking about football with Stephen.

"Do you have a bike?" Logan asked when we stepped outside.

"Of course I do," I replied.

Logan shrugged. "You never know. You may dance everywhere."

I didn't even give him the satisfaction of a response. Instead, I headed toward my garage, where the black-and-gray bike I've had since I was a kid sat, having collected dust since we'd moved. I strapped on my helmet and rode a circle around him.

"So where are we going?" I asked, curious about our next adventure.

"Don't worry about that," he said. "We just need to get moving. We have a very important group of people waiting on us."

When Logan and I entered the park a few blocks from my house, I spotted some boys from both the middle school and high school football teams. But while they stood together talking in a group near a picnic table, it was a group of tiny little humans that came running toward us. It turned out that the people counting on us were way shorter and way younger than what I'd expected.

"Logan! Logan!" the group of young boys yelled, as they surrounded us. Logan greeted each of them by name. The boys jumped up and down and were so happy to see him.

"Brooklyn, this is the Mighty Mites kindergarten team. They're some of the best football players in Leighton," he said as the kids grinned at him. "And, boys, this is my friend Brooklyn. Do you know who she is?"

My good mood instantly shifted. I bet he would introduce me as Tanner's sister. You could tell these kids were in love with football, and I was sure they were all fans of my stepbrother.

"Brooklyn is a ballerina. She dances on her toes," Logan said.

The boys' eyes got wide and so did mine. Logan didn't stop surprising me.

"But today we're lucky. Instead of dancing, she's going to play with us."

"Play?" I asked and raised an eyebrow at Logan.

Watching football, I could do. But playing? That was a whole different story.

"I've never played football in my life," I told him.

"But you now know how, after I taught you. And that's the next step to get you to respect the sport. If you play the game, you'll understand how much really goes into it. It's the same with ballet. I didn't appreciate how much work it was until I was actually dancing."

He did have me there. I may have understood the game, but participating was a whole different story.

Logan turned toward the boys. "What do you all think? Do you want Brooklyn to play with us?"

The boys cheered.

"What?" Logan asked. "I can't hear you."

The boys cheered even louder.

Logan turned to me. "Sorry, Brooklyn, the crowd has spoken. It looks like you're going to have to get your game face on."

I held my hands up to get them to quiet down.

"Okay, okay, I'll give it a shot," I said, which made them cheer louder. "But listen, I'm not promising that I'm going to be any good."

"You've got this," Logan said and pulled me over to the older boys and a few men who must have been dads. There were boxes of red and blue flags, and Logan handed a blue one to me. "You can be on my team. I'll talk you through everything. You have nothing to worry about."

"What exactly is all of this?" I asked as the rest of the group divided up.

"It's our weekly pickup game of football for the rec center. I played when I was their age and remember how awesome it was when the older football players joined us. So now I volunteer and play with them every Saturday morning."

My heart turned all warm and squishy inside as Logan talked about why he played with these boys. And they did look awfully cute, crowding around all the older players, all pumped up to play. Mia was right: Logan really was a nice person, and as crazy as it sounded, I was glad that he'd ended up being my partner. I would've never gotten to know him otherwise.

"I'm pretty sure they all love football," I said. "And it looks as if you're inspiring a whole group of mini-Logans."

Logan laughed. "That's my master plan. And then we'll take over the world," he joked. "So you're ready to show them what you've got?"

"I doubt I'll be any good. . . ."

"It's not about being good. It's about having fun, which is another reason why I love these games so much. The pressure is off to do anything but have a good time."

"Kind of like when Mary Rose lets us dance it out," I told Logan. When he gave me a puzzled look, I explained.

"A lot of times after a really long dance class where we've worked so hard we want to drop, she'll put on a popular song, turn it up, and we'll have one big fun dance party. It's not about positions or technique. It's about letting loose, being silly, and not caring what you look like."

"I love that idea," he said.

"Maybe we can dance it out after rehearsal one day," I teased. "I bet you have some hidden moves I haven't seen."

"Hey, I said I liked the idea. Not that I wanted to participate," Logan said, but he smiled. It would be funny to see what he'd look like. Just like it was going to be funny to see how I played football. Scratch that. Not funny, hilarious.

I followed Logan and a high school player named Colton to the huddle of little kids with blue flags. He got in the middle and began to give instructions to all of the boys. They gave their undivided attention to him, and I tried to follow what he was saying. My instructions were pretty simple. He assigned me to one of the kindergarteners on the other team and told me not to let him get past me if he had the ball.

"If he tries, grab one of his flags."

"Should I go easy on him?" I asked as the two of us headed toward the field.

"You won't need to," Logan said.

"Right," I said. "Like a group of kindergarteners are going to cream me."

"Just you wait," Logan warned with a grin that made me a tiny bit uneasy.

"Okay, sure," I told him and headed to the field. Marquis, one of Tanner's friends on the high school team, tossed the ball to another player, and the game started. It wasn't long before I realized Logan was right. These boys might be little, but they had a lot of heart and gave it their all.

I tried to guard the redheaded boy named Charlie who Logan had assigned to me, but it was impossible to stop him. He was fast, turning right, then left, then pivoting and running away from me. This happened after every single play.

Every single one. *Ugh!*

I couldn't stop the kid. I'd thought I was fast from ballet, but my skills were nothing compared to this boy's. One time he even turned around and stuck his tongue out and blew a raspberry at me as he ran away.

After chasing him around for twenty minutes, I was tired, exhausted, and having a blast. Each time a team scored, the kids on that team would break into these goofy chants that had everyone laughing. We took the game just seriously enough for a little friendly competition, but beyond that, it was a whole bunch of silliness.

"Why don't more of the boys on the team do this?" I asked Logan. "These kids are awesome!"

"They're missing out. I like to think of these Saturday mornings as my little secret."

"This is the best-kept secret," I told him. "And one of the best workouts I've had in a long time."

Logan nodded. "They may be little, but they're quick."

"I think I underestimated the skill of these kids. But this is where it ends. What Charlie experienced until this point was my warm-up. Now it's time to bring the thunder," I told him.

"The thunder?"

"Oh yeah, I'm done playing Miss Nice Girl. Charlie isn't getting past me."

I made my way back out to the field and stood in front of Charlie. I gave him the toughest face I could, which must not have been that good, because he busted out laughing.

"This means war," I said under my breath. I couldn't believe I was trying to play tough with a kindergartener, and if it weren't happening right in front of me, I wouldn't even believe it. But this kid wasn't getting past me again, so I slanted my eyes, curled my lips, and gave a snarl, in hopes that might make me more intimidating.

When the ball got passed to Charlie, I chased him

down the field, running as fast as I could. I reached my arm out and tried to close that extra space I needed to grab one of the flags that were flapping off of him. I was so close. So very close. I stretched my arm more and as I felt the plastic of the flag in my hand, my foot slipped on a wet spot of grass and everything slid out from under me. I lost my balance and skidded across the grass. The side of my foot banged against the ground, and oh my gosh, did it hurt.

I curled up into a ball and grabbed my foot. My ankle was throbbing, and it was impossible to keep the tears from coming out. The pain took my breath away. And that's from someone who knows what pain is. I dance on my toes, and my feet are covered in blisters and calluses, so when I say it hurts, you better believe I'm telling the truth.

I took my shoe off to relieve some of the pressure, and one of the little boys pointed at my ankle.

"Gross! Look at how big her ankle is!"

I glanced down, and he was right. It was huge and swelling by the second. It was almost double its size and was in fact pretty darn gross.

Most of the boys gathered around me and inspected my ankle with looks of disgust and fascination. *Great, I've become a science project.* I tried to slow my breath; my body was still on overdrive from my attempt to get the flag.

"Back up, please, and give me some room," a voice

said. One of the fathers kneeled down next to me. "Hi, Brooklyn. I'm Dr. Traina. Let's check you out and make sure everything is okay."

"Thanks," I said in a quiet voice.

"I'm going to take a look at your ankle. I'll be gentle, but let me know if I'm hurting you in any way."

"I'm tough," I told him, but right now, I didn't feel tough, especially when he picked my foot up to examine it. I clenched down on my teeth and told myself the pain would be over soon. The same as when I have to dance on a blister. It hurt for a moment, but once you pushed through it, the pain was forgotten.

"That's one banged-up ankle," Dr. Traina said. "You were moving fast when you fell, so you had a lot of momentum."

"Are you doing okay?" Logan asked. He bent down next to me, and I could see worry in his eyes.

"It hurts pretty bad," I admitted and swiped at a few tears that were on my cheeks, because why bother looking tough? Especially when I didn't feel like I was.

"Do you think you can stand?" Logan asked. He offered his hand to me, and I slowly stood up. It hurt to take a step, but I could do it, as long as I was careful.

"You probably want to have someone look at it," Dr. Traina said. "Just to make sure it's okay."

"I'm so sorry, Brooklyn," Logan said. "I thought this

would be fun. I didn't mean for you to get hurt. I hope this doesn't mess up your dancing."

"My dancing," I slowly said. I was so focused on getting Charlie and then falling, that I hadn't even thought about my dancing. My mind instantly went back to the recital, my sprained ankle, and how long I'd been out of dance.

What the heck was I thinking playing *football* today?

I couldn't believe I hadn't thought about how this might affect the Showcase.

I tuned out everyone around me. I couldn't think about anything except my ankle and the question that I didn't want to ask because the answer could be way too scary.

Tears rolled out of my eyes, and I didn't even bother to wipe them away. This wasn't the time to be tough. I couldn't, because what if I had done something? What if football really might ruin everything?

Chapter 36

D r. Traina suggested I have someone come and pick me up, since I wasn't exactly in the best shape to ride my bike home. That would have been a great idea, except when I went to call Mom, she didn't answer, which was a bit ironic since the reason she'd let me have a phone was specifically so I could get ahold of her when I had an emergency. Her phone went to voice mail, and the same happened with Stephen. I could call Tanner, but with everything that had happened with Mia and the video, I didn't really want to bug him to do me a favor. Sure, he said he was okay with everything, but I still felt bad bothering him on the weekend. But what other option did I have? I dialed his number on my phone and thankfully he picked up.

"Brooklyn?"

"Yeah, it's me. I'm sorry to bother you, but I was playing football with Logan and—"

"Wait, you were what?" he interrupted. "Did you say you were playing football?"

"Yeah, it's kind of a long story. I was with the Mighty

Mites, and I fell and messed up my ankle pretty bad. Mom and Stephen aren't answering their phone, so—"

"I'll come get you," Tanner interrupted, putting me out of my rambling misery. "Where are you?"

I told him the name of the park and not ten minutes later, I spotted his truck pulling into the parking lot. Logan waved him over and I tried to act tough, but that was next to impossible because it hurt so bad.

"Are you okay?" Tanner asked, and I shook my head.

"It really hurts. What if I've ruined everything? What if I can't dance?"

"We'll have Damien look at it, and then we'll deal with whatever comes next. I always find that's the best way to approach an injury, even though that can be easier said than done."

"Damien?"

"He's the team's trainer and my go-to guy when I get hurt. Even if it's something minor, he'll get you better right away. He's in on Saturday mornings, so we'll swing by and see if he can check out your ankle. I figured you might want to talk to him, since dancing is so important to you. I get how it is to be hurt and worried about how it's going to affect you."

"Are you sure he won't mind?" I asked, surprised that Tanner thought about me and ballet.

"Positive. He works with athletes all day long. He's the guy you want to see."

Athletes. I didn't say anything to Tanner, but it was incredible to hear him group me into that category. There were so many people who didn't look at dancers as athletes, especially in a town like this, where if you didn't play football, then you didn't need to bother playing a sport.

We pulled into the parking lot at the high school, and I turned to Tanner, worried. "He's really going to be okay with this?"

"He won't mind. We'll tell him you have an important performance coming up, and we need to make sure you're okay to dance."

There it was again. Tanner calling dance important. Of all the people I'd thought would respect ballet, he was one of the last ones. But people can sure surprise you sometimes.

Tanner used a key card to get into the athletic center of the school.

"Look at you with fancy VIP access," I said and thought about how cool Mia would think this was. I could practically hear her begging me to "borrow" the key card so she could get some inside scoop about what the locker room looked like or something. But as suddenly as that thought came, it left me as I remembered what Mia had done, and I was left feeling deflated.

"Some perks to being on the football team," he said, and I wondered what other things he was able to do.

Damien was the exact opposite of what I thought he'd look like. Instead of being big and full of muscles, he was skinny with long shaggy hair and wore wire-rimmed glasses. He had a bag of cheese curls open on his desk, where a computer sat with a video game paused on it.

"Tanner, my man, is everything okay?"

"Things are great with me, but not so much for my stepsister." Tanner explained to him what had happened, and Damien nodded as he talked. "So what do you think? Can you check her out?"

"Definitely. We'll see what we can do," Damien said and got up. He stretched his hand out to shake mine, but pulled it back when he saw it was full of cheese dust. He wiped it on his pants and stuck it out again.

"Sorry about that. Let's try this again. I'm Damien, and I'm your go-to guy to fix you up. So you hurt your ankle?"

I nodded and wonder how a skinny guy who ate cheese curls and played video games could work miracles on athletes, but if he could fix my ankle, I was willing to give it a shot. I was willing to give anything a shot if it meant I could dance.

"I sprained it really bad about a year ago and couldn't dance on it again for a long time. Then today, I was playing football and slipped on some wet grass.

"Those football guys are tough, huh?" Damien asked as he inspected my ankle and rotated it.

"Well, he was a kindergartener," I answered, embarrassed.

"That makes him even tougher!" Damien said. "Now, how does it feel when I move your ankle this way?"

"It hurts, but not as bad as it did when I first fell."

"Good, what about if I bend it back?"

He continued to ask me how different things felt, and when he was satisfied, he stepped back. "The good news is, everything is okay. You're going to have a nasty bruise that might impress some of those kindergarteners, but as long as you keep your foot elevated and iced today and tomorrow, you should be able to dance on it within the next few days."

"Really?" I asked as hope flowed back through me.

He held his hand out to help me off the table. "Brooklyn, you have specific orders from me to sit down on the couch and not get up unless you absolutely have to. Your prescription is nothing but rest, junk food, and movies. Do you think you can follow that?"

"That doesn't seem too hard," I told him.

Damien turned to Tanner. "You up for the job of making sure she does those things?"

"We'll stop on the way home and stock up on the important stuff; ice cream, candy, chips," Tanner promised him and gave him a little salute with his hand.

And that's exactly what we did. I waited in the truck while Tanner ran into the grocery store and came out with two big bags. When we got home, he brought a bunch of blankets and pillows into the family room, spread them out on the couch, propped my foot up on the table with a bag of ice over it, and proceeded to spread out everything he'd bought. Which, by the way, was pretty much any piece of junk food one could imagine.

"This isn't exactly the best pre-Showcase diet," I told Tanner. "And I'm pretty sure that if I finish all of this, I won't be able to dance ever again because my stomach will explode."

"Oh, it's not all for you," he said as he settled down on the couch and picked up a pint of ice cream. "I'm going to help you out. I figure it's my brother duty."

"It's your duty to eat all of this?"

"It's *our* duty to eat all of this. So what do you think? Chocolate chip or cookie dough?" He offered two pints of Blue Bell ice cream, and when I took one, he raised the other as if proposing a toast. "Here's to getting better in the best way possible."

The two of us hit our containers together and settled into our spots on the couch. I dove my spoon into the ice cream and took a giant bite, because chocolate made everything better, and I was most definitely in need of it right now.

Chapter 37

Three hours later, we had binge-watched way too much mindless television and made a serious dent in the food on the table.

And had a ton of fun.

I never thought I'd say this, but I had a blast hanging out with Tanner. And I wasn't sure why I hadn't made it a point to do it before this.

The two of us yelled at the TV together when the characters did something stupid, and we laughed so hard that at one point, we had tears coming out of our eyes. I'd always thought Tanner was into nothing but football and we could never find anything in common, but I guessed I was wrong. Because right then, he was pretty great.

And as much as I loved ballet, I thought about Tanner's words again, about not letting one thing take over your life. It was kind of nice to have a break from it without all the pressure and guilt, and just relax.

"I could get used to this," I told Tanner as I settled deep into the cushions. I thought about the afternoons I'd been spending with Jayden too and how much fun they were. "Maybe I'll give up ballet and become a professional couch potato."

"You could. It's okay to like more than one thing," Tanner said with a wink.

"Forget TSOTA. I'm going to spend my high school years on the couch binge-watching TV," I declared.

"Hey, there are worse things you could do," Tanner said. And maybe it was the sugar high, but for once, I didn't think it was so awful to have him as my stepbrother. In fact, I was thinking that I was pretty darn lucky to have him.

Chapter 38

It turned out that a weekend of junk food and television could do wonders for recovery. The swelling in my ankle went down within a few days, although I had to use crutches to keep any pressure off of it. Adeline begged me to let her carry my bag so she had another excuse to be late for class, and Jayden shared tips with me on how to walk with the crutches so my arms wouldn't hurt too much. Mary Rose advised me to stay off of it for the week to avoid making the injury worse, so instead of leading conditioning and taking dance class, I watched them.

Randy was the first to notice me when I entered the studio.

"What happened to you?" he asked in his usual blunt way.

"Football injury," I told him and smirked.

"Yeah right, and I got drafted into the NFL," he said.

"What team?" I asked. "Wait, let me guess. I bet it was the Cleveland Browns, because they're the only team desperate enough to take you," I said, remembering Logan's comments about how bad the team was.

Randy scowled and I gave myself an invisible high five for my comeback.

Logan came over and apologized again for what had happened, which was totally unnecessary.

"It wasn't your fault," I told him. "Besides, I loved playing football with those kids. And I plan to come back for a rematch. I just need to study some of your plays. I'm going to stop Charlie from getting the ball past me if it's the last thing I do."

"I'm sure they'd love to see you again too," Logan said. "And by the sound of it, I'm pretty sure a certain someone is starting to understand how much work football is."

"There is a lot that goes into the sport," I admitted.

"Wait, so you really did hurt yourself playing football?" Randy interrupted.

"I guess dancing isn't the only thing I'm good at. And if I were you, I'd hope you never have to play against me," I told him. "You don't know what you're up against."

I could tell Randy wanted to say more, but before he could, Mary Rose began class. The boys worked through all of her stretches and exercises, but when I wasn't dancing with them, it was pretty boring, so I hobbled outside to the waiting area.

Adeline and Elliana were already there, peering through

the one-way window into the studio. I should've known they'd come early to watch the boys.

"How is your ankle doing? Is it feeling any better?" Elliana asked.

"A bit. But I've learned it's really hard to use crutches and carry a big heavy book bag on your back. My armpits are killing me. These crutches were not made for comfort."

"Are you sure you don't want us to carry your book bag around?" Adeline asked. "Because I'm telling you, I will."

"I'm fine," I said. "You're going to have to find some other excuse to get yourself out of class."

"That's not why I'm doing it." Adeline pouted. "I'm offering out of the goodness of my heart."

"Sure," I said. "Keep telling yourself that."

"Speaking of the goodness of my heart," Elliana said, "I think I have an offer for you that you won't want to refuse. My sister got two tickets to the Thursday Evening of Art at TSOTA this week, and we can't use them. I asked my mom if I could pass them on to you, and she was cool with it. Do you think you'd want to go?"

"Yes! Of course!" I shouted without even giving it a second's thought. I couldn't believe Elliana was offering her sister's tickets to me. I had always wanted to go to their Thursday Evening of Art. It was held once a month, and tickets were by invitation only. Instead of tests and projects in the art portions of their classes, students presented their work for the month during Thursday Evening of Art. Each student got two tickets, and unless you knew someone who could hook you up, there was no other way to get them.

"I figured you'd say that. That's why I brought them with me."

She pulled out an envelope, and I clutched it to my heart. There was no way to begin to express to her how much it meant to me that she'd give me these. I hadn't been to a live dance show since that weekend with Mom. The familiar tug of sadness appeared, but before I could lose myself in it, I had a flash of inspiration. I'd ask Mom to go see this show with me. Maybe she didn't get to see me dance, but this show would kind of be the same. We could go out to dinner beforehand, and when we watched it, she'd remember that weekend we'd spent together. This might be the key to bringing Mom back to me. To making her remember how great it used to be with the two of us.

Chapter 39

I asked Mom about Thursday Evening of Art on the ride home. I was so excited that I couldn't wait.

"What do you think?" I asked. "You'll get to see the school in action, and we can go to dinner first. A girls' night!"

"I love the idea, honey," Mom said, and she smiled at me. "We could dress up all fancy and splurge on dessert."

"I like the way you think!" I told her, and it all sounded so amazing. I leaned my head against the back of the seat and closed my eyes, picturing all the fun we'd have that night.

My good mood was evident; both Stephen and Tanner noticed it, and while I told them it was because we had tickets to Thursday Evening of Art, the real reason is because *only* Mom and I had tickets. We would get a night to ourselves, and I was so excited about it that I was pretty sure I'd burst.

The rest of the week raced by in a blur, and nothing could get me down. Not even the thought of another rehearsal with Logan where he wouldn't be able to get the steps right.

"You seem especially happy today," Logan said when I showed up for rehearsal on Wednesday. Mary Rose had rescheduled it, since I had been hurt. It was my first time dancing again, and while Mary Rose had said we'd go easy, it still made me nervous.

"I am," I told him. "I'm very, very happy."

"Well, I'm about to make you feel even better," he said. He turned to Mary Rose, who was over by the music system. "Okay, let's show her the magic."

"The magic?" I asked, one eyebrow raised.

"Just you wait," Logan said. He grabbed a chair and pulled it up for me. "You may want to sit down for this. I'm just saying. It's probably going to shock you."

"Okaaaaay," I said, a bit concerned about what exactly it was I was going to see.

Logan walked to the middle of the floor and Mary Rose played with the sound system until the familiar sound of our pas de deux music filled the studio. Logan counted the beats with his fingers against his hip, and when he got to the sixteenth count, he began to move across the floor.

"Wait a minute," I said when I realized what was going on. "That's our dance!"

And it was. Logan was doing the footwork we'd tried to practice so many times. But unlike those earlier rehearsals, where he'd fumbled and tripped and messed things up, he wasn't doing any of that. In fact, he had every single step down.

About halfway through the dance, he gestured toward me.

"What do you think?" he asked, without missing a beat. "Want to give it a shot?"

I glanced at Mary Rose, who nodded. "You can mark it," she said. "Don't worry about dancing on pointe yet."

So I ran over to him, grabbed his hand, and we moved to the music. We mirrored each other step for step, and the only things we didn't do the complete moves for were the jumps. Instead, Logan counted the beats and would then pick right back up again with the steps. When the song ended, instead of standing next to him, I stepped aside and clapped as hard as I could.

"Bravo!" I yelled to Logan and Mary Rose did the same. "That was amazing! Where did that come from?"

"It was nothing," he said as if it were no big deal, when, in fact, it was a very big deal. "I've been practicing a little with Mary Rose."

I looked from him to her. "You two have been working together without me?"

Mary Rose nodded toward Logan. "He's the one who's been doing all the work. He's really been putting some time in to get the dance down."

I couldn't believe Logan had done this, especially when he was so busy with football. A wave of emotion welled up inside of me, and for a second I was afraid I was going to cry.

"Thank you," I said, even though those words didn't begin to express how thankful I truly was. He'd done this for me. Not because he'd had to, but because he'd wanted to. I remembered Mia's words when I hadn't wanted to dance with him. How she'd told me that he was a really nice person when you got to know him. She'd been right, and I was so glad that I'd listened to her, because if I had simply judged him based off of what I saw when he was with his friends, I would've never gotten to know him, and I would've missed out on so much. That idea made me think about Tanner, too, and how maybe, when you give people a chance, they can end up surprising you.

Chapter 40

If you would've asked me a month ago how life was going, I would've told you terrible. I'd lost my dance partner, my family was obsessed with Tanner and football, and I had to help with conditioning classes for a group of boys who acted more like animals than people.

But that was a month ago.

Now if you asked me how things were going, I'd tell you wonderful. Incredible. Stupendous.

"What's up with that goofy smile on your face?" Tanner asked as he drove me home from practice that night.

"Things are just going really good right now," I told him.

"Here's to awesome days," he said and held up his hand for a high five.

I slapped his hand and then reached out and turned up the radio. It was one of those roll-down-the-window-and-crank-up-the-radio type of nights. The kind where you didn't care if the wind messed up your hair, or if you couldn't sing one note on key. Tanner and I belted out the songs on the oldies station the entire way home.

The giddy mood from rehearsal still had me all amped up when we walked into the house. I waved at Mom and Stephen, who were in the family room watching TV.

"What's up?" I asked as I plopped myself onto the couch next to Mom. I peeked at the screen of her laptop, which she had balanced on her knees. "What are you doing? Online shopping again?"

"I wish," Mom said, and her voice held a sad note to it. One that most definitely did not match my good mood.

"Everything okay?" I asked her.

"Not really," she said and closed her laptop. "I wish I didn't have to say this to you, honey, because I know how much you were looking forward to tomorrow, but I'm not going to be able to go to Thursday Evening of Art with you."

And with that one sentence, my good mood vanished.

It was as if someone had whisked the carpet out from under me, and I'd crashed to the ground.

"Are you serious?"

"I'm sorry, sweetie, but tomorrow is parent-teacher conferences, and the other secretary is sick with strep throat. The school needs someone to run the front office, and unfortunately, I'm the only other secretary. I feel awful. Believe me, if I could get out of it, I would." She reached out and touched my shoulder, but I pulled away.

"Figure out a way," I told her. "Tell them that you already have plans. With your *daughter*."

"I tried," Mom softly said. "There isn't anyone who can do it. But we could find someone else to go with you. What about Mia?"

"Mia and I aren't talking," I reminded her.

"Isn't it time you two made up?"

"Not after what she did. I'm never going to forgive her," I said in a tone that made it clear there was no use arguing about it.

"Okay, what about one of your other friends? Or maybe Stephen could go."

"Never mind," I said. It was bad enough that she couldn't go with me; there was no way I wanted her to rattle off a list of my friends in hopes that one of them might have pity on me and go. It was pathetic and made things even worse. "I'll skip it. I'm sure someone else would love to go and take my tickets."

"Honey, you could find someone else," Mom said.

But why should I have to find someone else? I wanted to say. I was supposed to go with Mom.

"Forget it," I told her, even though there was no way I'd forget it. Not when Mom had once again chosen something else over me.

"I can go," Tanner said. I'd been so wrapped up in our

argument that I'd forgotten he was in the room. "I have practice right after school tomorrow, so I'm free in the evening. What if I took you, Brooklyn?"

"Um, I don't think you'd really enjoy it," I said. "It's all dance and music."

"Hey, I may not act like it, but I can be cultured too. Admit it: You take all of your etiquette tips from me," he joked.

"You mean the tips about leaving the toilet seat up and your wet towels on the bathroom floor?" I shot back.

"I'm simply showing you what not to do," he said. "But really, I don't mind going. You've gone to so many of my football games, I should see what this dance thing is all about too."

"Are you sure?" I asked, still skeptical.

"Positive. It will be fun."

"That's a great idea," Mom chimed in, and simply because I didn't want to hear about anything else she thought, I nodded at Tanner.

"Okay, sure. You can come," I told Tanner. "But you'd better not fall asleep like Malik did when he was at our recital this summer."

"What are you talking about? I love nothing more than hours of a classical concert or a night at the opera."

"Okay, you're pushing it a little too far now," I said,

and if I had been feeling a bit better, I probably would've laughed. Tanner was trying hard to make me feel better, and I was thankful for it. "The show is at seven, so we'll have to leave here tomorrow by six thirty. And make sure to take a shower."

"I'll be ready," Tanner promised. "And I'll take two showers. I'll be so squeaky clean that they'll have to tell me to quiet down."

"You're nuts," I told him, but I meant it in a good way. I was glad that I was still going to the show, but it was hard to be excited about something when the person I really wanted to spend time with couldn't make time for me.

Chapter 41

Tanner came downstairs shortly after six the following evening dressed as if he were going to some fancy, swanky event. He had on a suit, dress shirt, tie, and shined-up black shoes.

"Um, you do realize this is at a high school and not opening night at Lincoln Center, right?" I asked him.

"You can never look too good," he said and winked at his image in the hallway mirror.

"I guess it's better than your smelly warm-up jerseys," I told him.

"We both clean up well," he told me, gesturing to my own outfit.

"We do, don't we?" I said and grinned. I touched the sleeve of my dress. It was a pale pink, the color of my toe shoes. The top had a scooped neck and long sleeves, and the bottom was made of tulle and fell all the way to my ankles. It made me think of something a ballerina would wear onstage. I'd paired it with my white satin shoes that had tiny heels and a pearl bracelet Mom had given me for my tenth birthday.

Mom.

Even though I was grateful Tanner was going with me, the fact that she wasn't coming tonight still made my heart ache. And unfortunately, it reminded me way too much of how I'd felt the night she hadn't come to my recital, and that was something I never wanted to revisit again. If things had worked out the way they were supposed to, Mom and I would have been at dinner right now. We'd probably be deciding what dessert we should get, and maybe it would be too hard to decide, so Mom would say to pick two. We'd be having the best time talking and catching up with each other, since I hardly saw Mom anymore. Things would be like they used to. It was exactly the type of night I needed so desperately, but it wasn't going to happen.

"Earth to Brooklyn," Tanner said, and I snapped out of my daydream. "I asked if you were ready to go."

"Sure," I said and tried to sound enthusiastic, even if I wasn't.

The two of us headed out, and I was thankful when Tanner turned the radio on, so I didn't have to say anything. The music helped take my mind off of Mom not being here, and by the time we made it to TSOTA, my mood was a bit better. Maybe Mom wasn't here, but I was going to Thursday Evening of Art. And if I danced well at the Showcase, I might be a part of this one day.

It would be me that everyone would be coming to see.

I led Tanner into the school. I'd never been here before, but it still looked familiar. I recognized the main entry that led to the theater from the pictures of the website. The familiar stained-glass windows that stood on either side of the office looked amazing in the last of the evening light. Framed photos of graduates who'd gone on to work professionally in their specialized area hung on the wall. Their head shots smiled back at me, and below were plaques declaring what each of them were doing now.

JULIANNA LOWE——DESIGNER FOR MACY'S

JUIN-YE LING——ARTIST FOR PIXAR

SAMUEL FOSTER——FLUTIST IN THE CLEVELAND ORCHESTRA

CAMPBELL TANNING——SOLOIST IN THE SAN JOSE BALLET

I ran my fingers over Campbell's plaque. She was a legend at Center Stage Dance Studio. She had trained under Mary Rose ten years ago and landed a spot at TSOTA. She'd quickly begun to dance the lead roles in the Evenings of Art, and it wasn't long before she caught the eye of the New York Academy of Ballet. They offered her a spot there, but she chose to stay in Texas. Everyone thought she was making a mistake, but she was superclose with her sister and loved this school. It was a choice that proved to be the right one, because she was now a soloist in the San Jose Ballet. I watched her videos over and over again online and dreamed about having a similar story.

"Where do you think your picture is going to go?" Tanner asked, startling me out of my thoughts. I'd gotten so caught up in Campbell's story that I'd forgotten where I was.

"I have to get into the school first," I reminded him. "We're nowhere near picking out my space on the wall."

"Hey, there's nothing wrong with dreaming big," Tanner told me.

It kind of seemed silly to dream that big, but it was pretty great to know Tanner believed in me. Here he was cheering me on as if he were my biggest fan.

We wandered around the area by the theater a little longer. There was art set up all over: Pictures sat on easels, sculptures on small tables, and giant paintings hung on the walls. I examined each of them and imagined myself as a student here, until the lights flashed, indicating that the show was about to start.

Tanner put his hand on his hip with his elbow out to me. "Shall we?" he asked, and I linked my arm through his.

"We should," I agreed and the two of us headed into the theater and found our seats.

I loved every minute of the show. There were performances by soloists and ensembles of music and dance, and every part of it was amazing. The audience agreed, and we all cheered and clapped at the end of each performance. After one girl named Maddie did a solo on the piano where she played so fast, it looked as if her fingers were a blur, the entire room stood and gave her a standing ovation.

"Wow, she's really good," Tanner whispered, and I nodded in agreement. But also, somewhere deep inside of me a knot of fear and doubt settled. The dancers here were incredible. Some of them looked as good as the professionals that Mom and I had seen in *The Nutcracker*. Was I nuts to think that I could get into this school? I wasn't anywhere near as talented as these dancers.

The audience broke into applause and pulled me out of my thoughts. I gestured at them for Tanner.

"What do you think?" I asked him. "This is pretty much like being at a football game, right?"

"The funny thing is, this isn't too far off. Well, besides the fact that no one is painted up or wearing the school's colors."

"They're a little classier here," I said.

"Oh, that's the difference? Maybe I'll ask Leighton High to dress up for the next game. Everyone can wear their finest suits and formal dresses."

"I'd love to see that," I said and laughed, picturing everyone cheering the team on in heels and diamonds.

Tanner bumped his shoulder into mine playfully. "Thanks for letting me come to this with you. The stuff everyone here can do is pretty impressive."

"Thanks for agreeing to come with me," I said.

"I know I'll see you up there too," Tanner replied.

I closed my eyes and allowed myself to imagine that just might happen.

"That would be pretty wonderful, wouldn't it?" I asked and then thought back again to how good everyone had been up on the stage and how getting into this school did seem like making the impossible happen. "But it's really difficult to get in here."

"I've seen how hard you work. Plus, you're good. Nope, getting in isn't going to be the hard part."

"Then what is?" I asked.

"Figuring out how to get three tickets to Thursday Evening of Art instead of two, since I'm going to want to be sitting there right beside my dad and your mom cheering you on."

Tanner's words warmed me up inside. I loved that he wanted to come and see me dance at a Thursday Evening of Art, but I wondered if he'd ever get that chance.

Chapter 42

Mom apologized over and over again for missing Thursday Evening of Art, and while it wasn't her fault she'd had to work, there was still a part of me that was superhurt she hadn't gone. It hit too close to home and reminded me of the night she didn't show up for my recital. I think that was part of the reason why I still hadn't danced my solo for Mary Rose. She kept asking me to perform it for her, but something was holding me back, and I was pretty sure it had a lot to do with Mom. Dasha was the only one who had seen it since my horrible, awful recital, and I wasn't quite ready to perform it for anyone else yet, especially after watching everyone perform at Texas School of the Arts. I was so nervous something bad would happen again, but if I couldn't dance my solo in front of anyone, how did I ever expect to get into the school?

"Sooner or later, I need to see your solo. Regardless of whether you've danced it in the past, I can't let you do it in the Showcase without my approval," Mary Rose said, and I knew that she wasn't going to tolerate my stalling much longer.

"I'll dance it. I just want to work on it a little more myself," I told her, which was the excuse I'd been giving her this entire time.

"It would be good to give me some time to work with you on it. We want to make sure your technique is solid," she said.

"I'm pretty sure that after Brooklyn and I perform our dance, all those scouts won't want to see any more," Logan joked. "They'll be convinced that she's the perfect dancer."

"I wish that were true," I told Logan.

"There is such a thing as being overconfident," Mary Rose said.

"I know, right? That's why we aren't letting our amazing dancing abilities go to our heads," Logan joked.

"Okay, you two. Let's try the end of the dance again. I think you've almost got this double shoulder lift."

Mary Rose turned the music on, and Logan and I threw ourselves into the movements. The two of us had all the steps down, and everything seemed to go right. We were even able to do the shoulder lift without my wobbling or being afraid Logan would drop me. We had been working on that move for what felt like forever. It had been tough going for a while, as in I got dropped on the floor more than once and had bruises all over, but finally, we did it!

The two of us stood in shock.

"Did we just do what I think we did?" Logan asked.

"Do you mean danced better than we ever have before?"

"Um, yeah. That was pretty awesome. We conquered that lift. It looked as if you were flying."

"I felt like I was," I told him.

"I never knew how hard it was to do that. You all make dance look effortless."

"If it looks easy, that means we're working hard." I loved that he got it. Dance took a ton of work, and most people never even realized it.

"I think you two have this down," Mary Rose said. "Logan, you might be able to fool these talent scouts into thinking that you've been dancing for years."

"Maybe you should let them know you're interested in being recruited too," I joked. "Although I'm not sure I want to compete with you over one of the spots."

"You're totally onto something," Logan agreed. "Forget football—I'm going to be a ballerina."

"Ballerina or not, you two are ready for this," Mary Rose said, and maybe she was right. Maybe these doubts that kept sneaking into my mind were silly. Maybe we could do this. And that was amazing. It was the type of news I'd share with Mia. I was dying to tell her how we just might pull this off, but then reality crashed back into me. I couldn't tell her. We weren't talking. For a moment, I thought about texting her and telling her that I accepted her apology. I missed her, that was for sure, but I couldn't shake the awfulness of what she'd done to me, and I wasn't ready to forgive and forget.

"We're going to rule the All-City Showcase!" Logan said and pumped his fist in the air. "Those judges won't know what hit them when we get onstage. I wouldn't be surprised if they named the school after you."

I couldn't help but laugh. "I'm not sure about that, but I do feel good about getting into the school. And it's because of you. Thanks again for agreeing to be my partner."

"Hey, remember, it's helping me, too. Coach Konarski mentioned my improvement again the other day ago, and I was able to cut two more tenths off of my forty-yard dash! I'm almost at 5.4 seconds!"

"That's great!" I said, happy this was working for both of us. "Wait until Coach sees you twirling across the field with the ball!"

"Oh, yeah! It'll be our team's secret weapon!" Logan took off across the studio doing his version of split leaps. He was making a joke out of them, flinging his arms out, but this time I didn't get angry. I knew this time, he wasn't making fun of me.

Logan pretended to be an announcer as he spun. "The defense doesn't have a chance! Logan is twirling across the field with the greatest of ease! He's unstoppable! Look at him go!"

He moved across the length of the studio and spun right into Randy as he walked through the door.

Logan tried to stop, but the spinning had made him dizzy, so he grabbed the wall to try to center himself.

"Logan?" Randy asked, confused at first, but then he saw me and Mary Rose and began to put two and two together. "Are you taking classes here?"

"No," Logan quickly said, which was technically true, but I had a hunch that's not what he wanted Randy to think.

"Then why are you here?" Randy asked, not buying it for a minute.

"I'm here because Brooklyn needed help. . . ." He swept his arm around the place like it would explain something, but then slowly let it fall back down.

His face gave it away. He was embarrassed to be here. Embarrassed to be seen rehearsing with me. It might be okay to tell his family what he was doing, but when it came to Randy it was a whole different story. He had no intention of owning up to him about it. And that was not cool.

"Hey, it's all good," Randy said and headed toward the

lost-and-found box Mary Rose kept in the corner. Usually, it was full of mismatched socks and leg warmers, but Randy pulled out a red sweatshirt and held it up. "I forgot this after our last conditioning class, and my mom was on my case about making sure it didn't go missing. If I would've known you were going to be here, I could have asked you to pick it up after your ballerina classes. Anyway, it's nice running into you."

"Randy," Mary Rose said firmly, catching on to what he was doing.

Randy headed out the door but stopped and spoke to Logan again. "I hope you're not thinking of leaving the team to take up dancing. I don't want to hear about you ditching your shoulder pads for tights."

I opened my mouth to give Randy a piece of my mind, but closed it. This was between the two of them. I wished that Logan would stand up to Randy, but that didn't happen. In fact, right after Randy left, Logan followed as he mumbled some lame excuse.

I was left wondering what the heck had happened when not even ten minutes ago, we had been talking about ruling the world with our dancing.

Chapter 43

School for the next few days was awful. Logan avoided me, and I avoided Mia. And you better believe that lunch is no fun when you're not with your best friend. There's no one to watch online videos with or wonder what our favorite lunch lady, Mrs. Wamelink, looks like without her hairnet. I sat with Elliana and a few of her friends, and while they were nice and all, it wasn't the same.

I finished my salad but was still hungry, so I got into the lunch line to grab an apple. Logan, Randy, and a few boys from the team ended up behind me.

I smiled at Logan, and he nodded at me but then looked away. Something was going on, and I had a hunch that it had to do with Randy finding him in the studio yesterday.

I wasn't about to deal with them, but then Randy spoke up in that loud voice people use when they want to make sure that you can hear them, even if they're talking to someone else.

"Better lay off the cookies, Logan. You want to make sure you fit into those dance tights."

"I don't wear tights," Logan mumbled.

"Tights, tutu, whatever, you need to be light on your toes," Randy said and began to laugh as if he'd said the funniest thing in the world. Which, news flash, he hadn't.

I pretended I wasn't listening, because I didn't want to make things worse for Logan, but what Randy was saying was ridiculous and the rest of the team knew it. Anthony was the only other one who laughed; the rest of the boys didn't seem to think Randy was funny, which made me feel a little better.

"Hey, Brooklyn," Randy said, dragging me into a conversation I most certainly did not want to be a part of. "What do you think? Shouldn't Logan be in tip-top shape for all that twirling he's doing?"

"You're being a jerk, and you know it," I told him.

"Brooklyn . . . ," Logan said softly to get me to stop, but there was no way I was going to let Randy make a joke out of dancing. I was sick of them acting as if football was the be-all, end-all sport.

"There's nothing wrong with what Logan's doing. He's helping me out and getting some extra practice in while he's at it."

"Practice? Is that what you call it? I didn't know he'd be dancing around on his tippy toes on the football field," Randy said.

"He's a better player than you'll ever be," I told them. "Maybe instead of making fun of other people for trying to improve themselves, you should spend that time on your own skills. Because I've been learning more and more about football lately, and from what I've seen with you boys, there's still a lot of room for improvement."

I stepped out of the line and headed back to my seat. I wasn't hungry anymore, especially after the sour taste Randy had left in my mouth.

Chapter 44

I raced out of class at the end of the school day to find Logan. I needed to talk to him and told him as much when I spotted him walking down the front steps.

"Hey, sorry about lunch," I said. "I didn't mean to start anything there. I just hate the way Randy always puts down ballet, even after all the time he's spent at the studio."

Logan adjusted his book bag on his shoulders and walked a little faster, as if he didn't want to be seen with me.

"Is everything okay?" I asked as I tried to keep up with him.

"Not really," he said. "Randy's been giving me a hard time nonstop since he discovered me at the studio with you. Most of the other guys are cool with it, but Randy is relentless and has pulled some of the other guys into it."

"I don't understand," I said. "Randy talks like ballet is the worst thing ever, but every single boy on the team is playing better on the field because of the classes. Tanner even said that Coach Trentanelli was impressed with your improvement. It's stupid. Why does it have to be one way or the other? Why is ballet such a bad thing? You know how hard we work. It's as much a sport as anything else is."

"There's more to it," Logan mumbled.

"What more could there be? Ballet is tough. Dancers are strong. And if you think it's only for girls, then get over it. I'm pretty sure I'm as strong as some of those boys, and I'd love to see them dance in toe shoes and do fouetté turns. That way of thinking is plain stupid."

"I know," he said. "But some of those guys don't understand it the way I do."

"Then explain it to them. Help them see the work that goes into ballet. Just like you did with me and football."

"It's not so easy." He groaned in frustration.

Across the parking lot, a car beeped, and Mom waved out the window.

"My mom's over there. Do you want to get a ride to the studio?" Mary Rose had planned extra practices in the middle of the week, since the Showcase was so soon. Things might not be great with Logan right now, but I was hoping that once we got to the studio, it would all work out.

"About that . . . ," Logan started. "I don't think I'm going to be able to practice with you."

"You can't practice today?"

"I don't know, Brooklyn. I want to help you, I really do, but the team. We have to be united and work together. I was doing this to get better at football, but now it's all worse."

"Ignore it. Randy doesn't understand."

"It's not that easy. I'm around the team all the time. You know how important football is to me."

"And you know how important the Showcase is to me."

"I'm sorry. I keep trying to figure out what I can do to fix things, and I have no idea."

"I do. Stand up to Randy and tell everyone that this is dumb." Logan had me all fired up now. I got It—he didn't want the boys laughing at him, but there had come a point where he'd have to deal with it. "I can't believe you'd let one guy on the team control you like that."

"I'm not letting him control me. It's complicated," he said.

"The only complicated thing here is you backing out of a promise you made."

"Let me think about it. Okay?"

"Sure, think about it," I said. I tried to hide the panic in my voice, but it was impossible.

Chapter 45

I went to our practice even though Logan had said he wasn't coming. Logan had been pretty serious about taking a break, but there was still a teeny tiny part of me that thought maybe he'd show up.

I imagined him waiting for me in the studio like he always did. He'd be on his phone, playing his favorite game, the one where you had to get coins, and he'd grumble if I made him stop in the middle of it.

But of course, that was wishful thinking. When I walked in, the only person there was Mary Rose.

She was picking up the long ribbons she used with the little kids in their class, so I went over and helped her.

"About your dance," she said. "I want to work on getting a little more height on the lifts with Logan. He's got the strength to hold you, but he's still a little shaky."

I listened to her go over what she wanted to try with the two of us and wished that it was really going to happen. That Logan would magically appear out of thin air and be ready to dance.

"I don't think Logan is coming today," I finally told her.

It was hard to say it, to put the words out there, because it made it all seem even more real.

"He's not? Is he sick?" Mary Rose asked, her face filled with concern.

"Something like that," I mumbled, not wanting to tell her that Logan was too embarrassed to be seen with me. It was bad enough that Logan was choosing his football friends over me—I didn't need Mary Rose to feel sorry for me too, and that's definitely would she'd do if I told her the truth.

"Well, hopefully he'll be back soon," she said, her voice bright and cheery—the exact opposite of what was going on inside of me. "Do you want to run through it together?"

"If it's okay with you, I'm going to work on it myself."

"Of course. Let me know if you need help with anything. I'll use this time to see if I can get some of the mess in my office cleared up."

Mary Rose grabbed the last of the ribbons and left me alone. Only half of the lights were on, and they gave the studio a kind of magical glow, as if I were sleeping or in a dream.

I plugged my phone into Mary Rose's sound system, found the music for my solo, and let the opening measures wash over me. Hearing the music in what had become my new studio felt odd, like if I danced it here, I'd cross some kind of invisible line that divided my two worlds: the one before the move and the one after.

I closed my eyes and let the music fill my body so it almost became a part of me. The notes were etched on my heart, and I could sense them deep within me. I listened to the familiar music and remembered all of the good and all of the bad memories that this song held within it. Did I really want to dance it again? Did I really want to put myself through the pain from the last time? If I can't even dance it here, how will I be able to do it at the Showcase?

But what if I nailed the dance? What if I made it something wonderful?

But what if I didn't? Those dancers at Thursday Evening of Art were incredible. Could I ever compare to them? Maybe I'd be happy if I just danced and took classes at Center Stage Dance Studio. I could prepare for the Juilliard Summer Dance Intensive and not worry about the solo. Or even discover something new to do instead of dance. After all, Tanner had been able to do that. That would be okay, wouldn't it?

The song ended, and after a few seconds, I heard the notes start again. Mary Rose must have the repeat button on, something she does when she's going over a dance multiple times.

Just try it out, the little voice inside of my head whispered. *You're all alone here. No one is watching.*

And that's exactly what I did. I only hesitated for a moment before I let go of all of my doubts and fears. I launched myself into the dance, which I had first learned for Mom.

But here, in this studio, I wasn't dancing for Mom. I wasn't dancing for the audience that had been there that night. I wasn't dancing for Mary Rose or the scouts at the All-City Showcase. I wasn't dancing to prove myself or make someone notice me. I didn't worry about who might be better than me, or if I could compete with the other dancers at TSOTA. I danced for only one person.

I danced for myself.

I let the music carry me away until the world around me disappeared and I remembered how good it felt. My body craved this, and I pushed myself to jump higher, extend straighter, and reach farther for no one but myself. I danced purely for the love of it, and it was incredible.

When the song ended, I fell to the floor and stretched out my arms and legs, almost as if to make a snow angel. I focused on the ceiling and tried to get my breath to slow. My lungs worked overtime to suck in air, my muscles ached, and my legs trembled slightly from the exertion of dancing.

And I loved it.

"You were awesome," I whispered to myself, because this song had reminded me that when it came to dance, I was the only person who mattered.

omeone began to clap as I lay on the floor trying to catch my breath. I raised my head as Mary Rose walked into the room. Heat instantly rushed to my face as I realized that she had caught me dancing.

And not just dancing, but dancing my solo.

"How much of that did you see?" I asked her.

"Enough to know that if that isn't your solo, you need to make it your solo," she said.

"Do you really think so?" I asked.

"Brooklyn, I know so. That was incredible." Mary Rose came over to me and sat on the floor where I was. "It's none of my business to ask why, but it's evident that you're avoiding dancing that solo for some reason. I'm telling you right now that you don't need to worry about it. Dance your solo and don't worry about anything else but feeling the music like you just did."

I played with the ribbon on my toe shoe and decided to confess the truth to her. After all, she had already seen the dance, so what harm could it do now? "That's the dance I was performing when I hurt my ankle. I'm fine now, but

I can't stop thinking about that night. I'm afraid that I'm not going to be able to pull it off and I'll hurt myself again"

Mary Rose nodded. "It's always hard to try something unfamiliar or out of your comfort zone, but trust yourself. You've got this. I've seen a lot of dancers go through this studio, and you have something special. Believe in that and you'll do an amazing job."

"I'm not sure I can do that," I confessed. "My mind gets so full of self-doubt and fear."

"Don't think about anything. At all," Mary Rose said. "That's the secret. Don't dance for anyone except yourself, and if you do that, you'll be perfect. It's when you let those other thoughts creep in that you mess yourself up."

I thought about how I had just danced my solo for myself and no one else. How I hadn't cared about who was watching me and how amazing it felt. Maybe that's the secret to an incredible performance all the time.

"So I dance for myself?" I asked her.

She smiled in a way that made me feel as if I had said just the right thing. "You always dance for yourself," she told me. "Always."

Chapter 47

The days moved past, and as each one ended, so did a little more hope that Logan would change his mind. And as good as I felt about my solo, I still believed that without Logan, my shot at getting into TSOTA wasn't going to happen.

I saw him a bunch of times at school, laughing and joking with his friends, but he avoided me like I was radioactive, and he hadn't shown up for the conditioning class or our last two rehearsals. I made up a lame excuse about him being sick to explain to Mary Rose why he wasn't there, and I went through the motions at class, but my heart wasn't in it. I was going to have to tell her the truth soon, and the thought of that made everything freeze up inside of me.

I thought about trying to talk to him again, to reason with him, but then I pictured the way he had looked after Randy found him in class and knew it was no use. Logan loved football too much; I didn't stand a chance.

I tried to make myself feel better. I told myself that I could be like Tanner. Dance didn't have to be my life. There were a million other things that I could discover. Mia loved creating her vlogs; maybe I could help with that. Or I could check out the drill team or even cheerleading. I reminded myself that it was okay to like other things and that maybe this was for the best. Maybe I'd discover that I loved something completely different that I never, ever would have given a chance if it weren't for everything that was happening.

I tried to keep myself busy and hung out with Jayden both at school and at home; the two of us watched a ton of bad television, ate a bit too much candy, and played about a million board games. While it was great to spend time with him, it wasn't enough to destroy the gray cloud of gloom that sat above me.

I was in math class on Thursday when my classmates began to whisper. I turned toward the front of the room to see what the commotion was, and Logan stood in the doorway.

And not just Logan, but Logan and a giant mum.

It was the biggest and gaudiest mum I'd ever seen.

Mums are one of the strangest parts of Texas culture that I've experienced. When I first moved here, there were a lot of things people did that I had to get used to, like worshipping Friday-night lights, slow-cooking your meat for hours, and displaying the Texas flag everywhere. More often than not, I felt as if I were living in a different country, not a different state. Texans had their own code for everything, and while some of it didn't make complete sense, I accepted it as something that was part of the culture. But the one thing I couldn't quite figure out was mums.

Mom had spent the last week working on one for Tanner's homecoming date. When she first began to talk about making the perfect mum, I was completely confused.

"Can't you order them from the florist? What's so hard about that?" I had asked.

"Mums are not flowers," Mom said, as if that was helpful. Which, obviously, it wasn't.

"Mums *are* flowers. The ones you used to buy in the fall to put outside on the porch."

"We're talking about homecoming mums," Mom said. "They're completely different."

I have no idea how Mom became the expert on these so-called mums, but she was right. When I Googled images of them, I couldn't believe what I saw. They were a tradition that happened during homecoming in Texas, where the boys would make these giant things that the girls would then wear. They kind of looked like ribbons you'd win, with a round circle the size of a plate in the middle and decorations hanging off of it. Girls wore them around their necks because they were too big to pin onto their clothes. When it came to mums, the motto definitely seemed to be the bigger the better. There were pictures of ones that stretched all the way to the ground, and the fancier ones had stuffed animals, glitter, and lights on them.

Mom was going all out with the one she was making, and by the look of things, I was pretty sure it wasn't going to disappoint. It had Tanner's date's name, Carley, across the front in a heart with strings of beads and probably about ten pounds of ribbons hanging off of it. Mom had sewn a ton of sequins all over so it flashed like a disco ball when it moved. I had told her that she might have gone a little bit over-the-top, but she'd said she wasn't done with it. She needed to add more glitz. I don't know what it was about these mums, but they seemed to make people go crazy. Crazy with a capital *C*.

But what was crazier was the humongous one that Logan now held as he called my name.

The entire class turned to stare at me.

I raced to the door to get him to stop.

"What are you doing?" I asked after I'd pulled him outside and down the hallway a little bit to make sure no one could see us from inside the classroom.

"I made this for you," he said, and to his credit, he looked pretty proud of that fact.

"For me?"

"Yep, this is your mum."

"Um, okay," I said and studied it. The mum was bigger than any I'd ever seen before. He had to carry it with two hands, and it covered almost the entire front of his body. It was a giant circle, easily bigger than a basketball and surrounded in row after row of tulle. There were twinkle lights hanging down from it, along with enough satin ribbon to wrap Christmas gifts for every child in the world. I was pretty sure there had to be a shortage of ribbon now in the state of Texas. And in the middle, in giant glitter letters, were the letters TSOTA.

"Shouldn't it say LMS?" I asked.

"This mum doesn't represent Leighton Middle School, it's for Texas School of the Arts. I figured you could wear it to celebrate when you get in."

"In case you forgot, I'm not going to get in. I lost not one, but two partners. Pretty sure I'm cursed. My chances of getting noticed at the Showcase are slim to none." I gave Logan the meanest look I could, because, come on, this was ridiculous. What did he think he was doing? He'd already ditched me, why make things worse?

"That's where you're wrong. You lost one of your partners. I might be stupid and think about myself in selfish ways, but I've come to my senses. And I'm asking if I can be your partner again."

Logan waved the mum around like it was dancing, and I about died from embarrassment. I couldn't believe he'd made that awful, giant mum.

"That thing is ridiculous—put it away," I said.

"Well, yeah, that's the problem. This thing is pretty hard to hide."

"Why did you make one that big?"

"Isn't it obvious? I want everyone to know that I'm dancing with you in the All-City Showcase."

"Even your football team?" I asked, my eyes narrowed.

"*Especially* my football team," he said. "Listen, I was awful. I let those guys get to me. But it won't happen again. I made a promise to you. I like dancing, and we're good. If the guys on the team can't see that, it's their loss."

"Pretty sure they're going to see that," I told Logan as I pointed at the mum.

"That's the idea. But I don't care. I realized how stupid I've been and how important ballet really is for the both of us."

"Ballet is important to you?" I asked.

"You're not going to believe this, because I hardly can, but Coach Trentanelli came to our practice the other day. The pressure was on big-time, but sometimes I work better under pressure, if that makes sense. Anyways, we ran a bunch of drills and guess who did a forty-yard dash in 5.4 seconds?"

"Oh my gosh! Did you really?" I said, my excitement for Logan overtaking any anger I had for him at the moment.

He grinned so big I could see his molars. "Yep! And not only that, Coach Trentanelli explained the postseason training and asked if I was interested. I'm going to get to practice with the high school team this winter!"

"That's amazing! I'm so happy for you," I told him, because I knew there was nothing Logan wanted more than to be a part of the high school team.

"I still have to show him more progress the rest of the season, but I figure if I stick with ballet, I can only get faster. And that's all thanks to you."

"You earned it," I told him. "I had nothing to do with it."

"You helped. Ballet helped, which is why I'm coming back to you right now to say sorry. The way I treated you was wrong. It was stupid of me. You're an athlete too. You're pretty much obsessed with ballet, but in a good way. Your dedication made me want to work just as hard at football."

It was nice to hear Logan say those things, but I was still hurt about his leaving me hanging. "The way you treated me wasn't fair. It was awful."

"I *was* awful, I admit it," Logan said sheepishly. "I let some of the other guys on the team make me feel a certain way, and that was dumb. They're the stupid ones not being open to new things and giving ballet a shot. I'll try anything now, because imagine what else I can improve on. I'm pretty sure the superhuman speed I have today is only the beginning."

"Superhuman speed?" I asked and held back a laugh.

"Pretty much. I'm like a cheetah," Logan said and grinned, but then his face turned serious. "I mean it, Brooklyn. I'm sorry. I promise I won't let you down again. I'm in this until the end. If you decide to forgive me, there's no getting rid of me, even if you want to. So what do you think? Will you accept this mum and let me dance in the Showcase with you?"

There was a little voice in the back of my mind telling me that I shouldn't forgive him. Was it smart to trust him again after what he'd done? But he looked so hopeful and silly with that mum, it was hard not to give him another chance. Besides, he was my only shot at getting noticed at the Showcase. I needed him to be my partner.

"Okay," I reluctantly agreed and hoped I wasn't making a mistake. "But I want you to carry that thing around today for me. And when people ask why, you have to tell them the truth."

"Oh, you better believe that I will," Logan said. And he put the giant mum around his neck. "Now what do you say we go back into class and show this thing off!"

"You do know there's boys from the team in there?" I asked.

"Hey, I can't help it if they get jealous," Logan said and gestured to me to follow him. He strutted into the room, showing off my mum like it was the greatest thing in the world, which it kind of was. And the best part was that I had my partner back and the two of us were going to rock the All-City Showcase.

Chapter 48

Not only was Logan at our conditioning class after school, but he showed up with that awful, giant mum around his neck. And instead of avoiding me when I came into the room, he waved his hands wildly around to get my attention.

"There she is," he said, his voice so loud that it filled the entire room. The rest of the team stopped what they were doing and stared. My face instantly heated up at the attention that was now on me. "My dance partner is here."

Wait, what? Was Logan serious? Was he really calling me out in front of all his teammates? The same teammates that had made him quit being my partner? I waited for Randy to crack a joke or act like the same immature boy who had been giving him a hard time about dancing with me, but it didn't happen.

"Um, have aliens invaded the studio? What have you done with the football team?" I asked all of them when they remained silent.

"It's okay, Brooklyn," Logan said. "I talked to everyone, and it's all good."

"Everything is not good," I said and focused on Randy. I thought about how awful he'd been to me and how unfair it had been to make Logan feel as if he were doing something wrong. "Maybe you're all cool with us dancing together now, but a few of you seem to have had a lot of fun giving Logan a hard time about helping me out."

"It wasn't right," Anthony spoke up. "Especially since you've done nothing but work with us to become better football players."

"And we *are* becoming better players," Logan said and turned to me. "Which is what I explained to everyone. We are so thankful for everything you've done. If it weren't for you and ballet, we wouldn't be playing the way we are. You've helped us get to this point, so I told them that if someone has a problem with me helping you, then maybe they need to stay out of the studio."

"I think that sounds like a very good idea," I said, as I looked straight at Randy, who focused his gaze down at the foor instead of on me.

"Logan told us about how much the two of you rehearsed and about all the extra practice you do beyond that. You're super dedicated," Jimmy said. "That's a lot of work."

"It is," I agreed. "But I love it, so it isn't like I'm working."

"Like football," Logan said. "Which makes sense. Ballet is a lot like football."

"Ballet is like football?" Randy asked, and scowled. But he had the other boys' interest.

"Hear me out," Logan said and held his hand up to stop the boys from agreeing with Randy. "When you're in a game, you have specific plays that you do in order to move the ball down the field. Strategy is everything in football, and if you can't execute your plays, your team will lose. Just like you rehearse a dance, we rehearse these plays. We watch film, we do mental reps, and practice them with the team on the field nonstop until they become second nature. That way, when Coach Konarski calls a specific play, we know exactly what to do. It sounds nuts, but it's just like dancing."

"That does sound nuts," Jimmy agreed with him, but he nodded as if it made sense.

"When you break it all down, football is really one big dance. You just have to hope you execute it better than the other team," Logan said.

"I guess you could look at it that way," Jimmy agreed slowly, which must have blown his mind because never in any of these boys' wildest dreams did they probably ever think that we'd be able to look at football and ballet on mutual ground.

Anthony spoke up, "And your dance for the Showcase is a lot like our team trying to make it to the playoffs. And the championship for you is Texas School of the Arts."

"It is," I said. TSOTA was everything to me.

"We understand why Logan is dancing with you," Anthony said. "Why he *needs* to dance with you. We didn't mean to mess up your chance to get into the school. Especially after everything you've done for us."

"Thanks," I told them and then focused on Randy. "You're okay with this too?"

Randy shrugged. "Logan's right. You work hard."

It wasn't exactly an apology, but from Randy, any sort of acknowledgment was pretty major.

"It's one thing to say you're sorry," Logan said. "But we thought we'd *show* you how sorry we are."

"You're going to show me?" I asked. How exactly do you show someone you're sorry?

Anthony spoke up. "When Logan talked to us, he asked us to put ourselves in your shoes, so we did. It would be so hard to move to a new place where you don't know anyone. Ballet is important to you, so while we don't have those fancy pink shoes you use to stand on your toes, we asked Mary Rose to show us how to do a piqué turn."

"You did?" I asked, not believing him for a second. Piqué turns took some work to get right.

"Yep," Jimmy said. "We came in yesterday and worked with her. And now we're ready to show you our stuff."

Logan gestured toward the group of boys, and everyone lined up at one end of the room. Even Randy begrudgingly joined the group, although he didn't look too happy about it. Mary Rose, who had stood in the corner watching everything with an amused look on her face, turned on some music. And sure enough, one by one, each of the boys did piqué turns across the room. Well, most of them *attempted* to do them, while Randy didn't put much effort into it, but it was the thought that counted.

"You all did this for me?" I asked, and a whole bunch of emotions welled up inside of me. What they had done was so nice and unexpected.

"Yep, and it wasn't easy," Anthony said.

"Really?" I asked the group. "Are you saying that what dancers do is hard?"

"Not hard," Jimmy said. "*Impossibly* hard."

"We *all* work hard," I told the team. "Logan's taught me a lot about everything that goes into playing football."

"How about we agree that we're all pretty amazing?" Logan suggested, and the group nodded in agreement, but the thing was, he was right. The team might not totally get ballet, and I'll never love football the way that this town does, but I understood exactly what Logan meant about respecting one another and what we did.

Chapter 49

While the homecoming game was pretty much the biggest event of the football season at Leighton, the homecoming bonfire was a close runner-up. Mia had talked it up since the start of the school year, and it sounded amazing. The school brought in food trucks, got a DJ, and had tons of carnival games and smaller fire pits where you could roast hotdogs or marshmallows. Mia had planned to bring Reese's cups to use instead of chocolate bars. She swore by them, and I wasn't about to argue about that flavor combination. I'd been looking forward to the bonfire and we had hoped to get our parents to let us have a sleepover even though it was a school night. But after what Mia had done, none of that was going to happen now.

So instead, I headed to the bonfire with my family, and it wasn't the same. Sure, the hum of excitement was in the air, and there was definitely a fun party atmosphere going on. Teachers took turns sitting in the dunk booth, the drill team taught people a dance, little kids jumped in bounce houses, and Mom gave me money to spend on junk food, but there was something missing. And that something was my best friend.

I couldn't find Mia in the crowd, but I did see Logan with that ridiculous mum. It had been a week since he'd shown up outside my classroom with it. The bottoms of the ribbons were dirty and ratty now from being dragged all over the place. I couldn't believe he still had it.

"I'll have you know this is the most wanted mum out there," he said. "I already had three girls point it out to their dates, telling them that this is exactly what they want for the dance Saturday."

"Maybe I'll show it off myself and make everyone jealous," I said, because all was good now. He helped place it around my neck, and even though it weighed a ton, I wore it proudly.

I posed for him. "What do you think? Should I wear this for the Showcase?"

"Totally. You'd catch the eye of all the talent scouts in that."

"Right?" I asked, and the two of us cracked up.

"There's Mia," Logan said, pointing across the fire to where she stood with her microphone out to a girl in our grade. "I bet she's doing her on-the-street interviews. Should we see what question she's asking tonight?"

He headed toward her before I could say anything.

"Hey, Logan," I called, and he stopped. "The thing is, Mia and I aren't really talking to each other right now."

Logan stopped and turned around. "Isn't she your best friend?"

"She *was* my best friend," I told him. "All of that stuff she posted in the video about Tanner was private. I trusted her to keep quiet, but instead, she shared our conversation on her YouTube channel."

"Oh man, that's tough. I didn't know that was all a secret. I figured Tanner was cool with that video. But is it worth missing out on spending time with her?"

"What are you talking about? Of course it is. I had no idea she was even recording. She took our private conversation and used it like it was her news to share."

"That's not cool, and I'd be mad too, but the two of you were best friends. It's kind of like me and the football team. Once I talked to the team about all the ballet stuff, I felt so much better. And look at the two of us. Not only did you forgive me, but you got that amazing mum, too."

I rolled my eyes and played with the ribbons on the mum. What he was saying made sense, even if it wasn't easy. "It's hard to forget about what Mia did."

"You don't have to forget. But don't let it ruin things."

I stared into the giant bonfire and thought about all

the ways I'd missed Mia this last month. "Maybe you're right."

"Of course I'm right," Logan joked. He gave me a little push toward Mia. "Now go talk to her. Get this figured out so we can all hang together tonight."

I let the momentum of Logan's push move me forward. If he forgave the team for making fun of ballet, and I forgave him for getting cold feet about being my partner, then I should be able to make up with Mia, right?

She was finishing up her questioning of the girl when I walked up to her.

"Brooklyn!" she said, her voice a mix of surprise and happiness.

"Hey," I said. "Can we talk?"

"Sure, let me turn off this camera," she said, and I knew she was doing it for me. To make me feel better.

"No, don't," I told her. "I want you to record this apology. I should've forgiven you a long time ago. I miss you and want my best friend back."

Mia shook her head and held her hand up to me to stop. "Please, you're not the one who should be apologizing. I'm the awful one. I shared stuff I shouldn't have just to try and get more views, and that was stupid."

"It was pretty awful. You hurt me. I trusted you to keep that to yourself," I said, and it was good to get that off of my chest. To say the words I'd been thinking for so long.

Mia nodded. "I know. I didn't have any right to do that. I'm sorry. It won't happen again."

"Promise?" I asked.

"Cross my heart," Mia said.

"Then I think we should agree to move on."

"I like that plan."

"Well, on one condition . . ."

"Anything," Mia agreed.

"That you help me build some giant s'mores tonight."

"I can do better than that." Mia picked up the backpack she always carried with her camera equipment in it. She opened the front pocket and pulled out a bag full of Reese's cups. "I'll introduce you to the best s'more you've ever had in your life."

And that was the perfect way to close a deal.

"Best friends again?" I asked.

"Always," she said, and as the two of us sealed our friendship with a hug, Logan came over.

"Those Reese's cups are to share, right?" he asked.

"Yep! Now let's go test them out," Mia said, and the three of us set off toward one of the fire pits to pick the perfect spot to make our s'mores. And it felt so good to have my dance partner and my best friend with me again.

Chapter 50

We had Friday off because homecoming was basically a national holiday here. No, really, it's the truth. There was a big parade in the morning with the marching band, and the girls on the homecoming court rode through the streets in convertible cars and threw candy at the kids who cheered them on. Each team, all the way down to the Mighty Mites, rode on floats, and when the middle school boys came by, Mia and I cheered extra loud for them. They waved, and Logan pelted us with handfuls of candy.

Mom couldn't wait for the game and was dead set on leaving an hour early to get a good seat.

"You'd both better get down here fast, because I'm walking out this door in one minute," she yelled from the bottom of the steps.

I finished braiding my hair, grabbed a hooded sweatshirt, and ran out of my room. Most people only joked about leaving, but Mom was the type of person who actually would. There'd been a number of times when I'd missed rides to school and had to walk the seven blocks from our old house, because Mom doesn't like to be held up. So when she told us we had a minute left, she meant it.

Stephen and I narrowly avoided colliding in the hallway as we ran out of our rooms.

"Your mom doesn't cut us any breaks, does she?" he asked.

"Never," I said. "Once she told me we were eating, and I was five minutes late, and by the time I got to the table, she'd eaten all the French fries because she said I was too slow."

"That's so not cool," Stephen said.

"That's called making sure to be on time," Mom said, coming up behind us. "You snooze, you lose. Now let's get going."

We hurried out of the house, and it was a good thing Mom kept us moving, because even though we were an hour early, the stands were packed. It was hard to find a seat together, but luckily we were able to get a spot about halfway up next to Jayden and his parents. He'd just gotten his giant cast off and now had on a walking boot which made it easier for him to get around.

"Does this mean our weekly movie and game nights are ending, because I'm pretty sure this next week is when I finally beat you at Monopoly," I told him.

"Yeah, right, as if you could ever beat the master."

"Never say never," I said.

"Don't worry, I'm still sidelined for a few more weeks. Which means a few more weeks to remain the undefeated Monopoly champion."

"Hey, I'm simply going easy on you," I said and then gestured toward the stadium. "Speaking of undefeated, I'm pretty sure the entire state of Texas is here to cheer on Leighton."

I didn't think it was possible for the crowd to be any bigger than it had been at any other game, but tonight proved me wrong. It was so loud that I was pretty sure my ears would be ringing for days, and there was no way my earbuds would block out the noise tonight with my music. But the truth was that I didn't want to put my music on. Tonight I thought I'd pay attention to the game and give it a shot.

I was able to understand a bit of what was going on because of my time with Logan, and the energy from the crowd was contagious. I waved the flag in my hand as high as everyone around me and yelled so loud that my voice didn't stand a chance in sticking around past the first quarter.

Quarter! I smiled, proud of myself for remembering the word. Before Logan, I'd had no idea how long a game was or how many points a team could score.

"So if they kick this field punt, then we get two more points, right?" I asked Mom.

She smiled. "It's a field goal. And yep, we'll be in the lead."

Okay, maybe I wasn't a pro, but close to it. Close enough that when Jayden's brother Malik's kick sent the ball sailing through the goalposts, I jumped up with everyone and pumped my fist in the air.

"We're awesome!" I yelled.

Mia came up next to me right at that moment and caught me in a full-out Leighton love fest.

"This isn't so bad, is it?" Mia asked and smirked at me.

"You're right. It's kind of fun when you get into it."

Mia pulled out her phone and pretended to record me. "Can you say that again, please? I'm pretty sure a miracle has occurred."

I gave her a playful push and shook my head. "Come on now, let's not get too crazy. I'd still rather be dancing."

Her face changed for a split second, and the happy look in her eyes disappeared. "Of course you would. How could I forget?"

I couldn't tell if she was upset or joking, but I didn't have time to figure it out because the quarter ended and people around us began to stand to get food during halftime.

Mia held up her microphone. "I better go get some interviews while people are fixated on the game. I'll catch you guys later."

Mia ran off and Mom pointed to the bottom of the bleachers.

Mom nudged me. "I think you're wanted down there."

Tanner stood on the field and waved his hands at me.

"What does he want?" I asked her.

"I have no idea; go find out."

Jayden stood up and grabbed my hand. "Come on, I'll go with you. I'm always up for a good mystery, and we'll see how I can do with this boot," he said. I followed him down the steps, totally aware that most of the people in the stands around us were watching us.

"What's going on?" I asked Tanner when we reached the bottom.

"Put this stuff on," he instructed. He tossed a duffel bag up to us, and when I unzipped it, I discovered it was full of Leighton High stuff. Shirts, a big poufy red tutu to wear over leggings, hair ribbons, and even those giant foam fingers.

"Why?" I asked.

"Just do it. I only have a second," he said. "I need to go to the locker room, so be quick."

I eyed him suspiciously. I had no idea what he was up

to, but from the rushed look on his face, he wasn't going to give me time to ask. Jayden began to put a bunch of the clothes on, so I did the same. When we were dressed, Tanner gestured toward the other end of the bleachers.

"Okay, follow me," he said, and we had no choice but to do it, especially since it appeared we were the entertainment at the moment for those who had stayed seated in the stands.

Jayden shot me a look, but I shrugged and the two of us walked along the bottom of the bleachers as we followed Tanner. He took us all the way to the other end, where the student section was.

The high school student section.

Aside from being on the team and sitting on the players' bench, the student section was the most coveted spot in the stadium. You could only sit there if you were in high school, and even then, the seniors sat on the bottom while the lower classmen were stuck at the top. It was the rowdiest, wildest part of the stadium, and anyone who was anyone made sure to have a spot there.

"Those are your seats," Tanner said and pointed to an open spot on the bleachers, right in the middle of the craziness. The area was nothing but a sea of red and white. Kids were decked out from head to toe in the colors. Two rows below our spot was a group of shirtless boys with paint across their chests. They each had a white letter on them that spelled out LEIGHTON and did some chant where one of them would yell something and the rest would respond.

"No way," I said. "We can't sit there; we're not allowed. In case you forgot, Tanner, Jayden and I aren't in high school."

"Maybe not, but you're my little sister. And I don't usually play the quarterback card, but this is a good time to do so. Logan filled me in on how he's been teaching you about football, so I think it's time you have the ultimate fan experience." Tanner turned toward the crowd in the student section and cupped his hands so that he was making a megaphone with them. "What do you all think? Is it cool if Brooklyn and Jayden sit here with everyone?"

The student section went wild. Everyone cheered and welcomed us into their group.

"There you go," Tanner said. "It looks as if the crowd has spoken. No one is going to give you any trouble. So go and have fun."

He gestured to the seats and gave one more wave to the crowd before heading down. Everyone stomped on the bleachers, and the ground below me vibrated. Tanner really knew how to get everyone revved up.

Jayden sat down, waved one of the foam fingers that Tanner had given us, and grinned at me.

"This doesn't mean that I've gone over to the football dark side, but it is pretty cool to sit here. Your brother rocks," he said.

"Step—" I started but stopped. Why did I need to correct everyone? Was it that important? Instead, I smiled back at him. "He is pretty cool, isn't he?"

The excitement of the student section was contagious, and I quickly found myself dancing and chanting as loud as everyone around us. The sun sank down, and with the stadium lights shining onto the field, the music from the band, the shouts from the crowd, and the cool breeze in the air, the night had a sort of magic to it. Like this was exactly where I wanted to be at this moment.

Chapter 51

It seemed like it would be impossible for the town to get any crazier about the football team, but it was happening, and I was swept right up with them. Leighton High finished the season undefeated and then blew through the playoffs, eliminating every team placed in their path until suddenly they were headed to the championships, with Tanner leading it all.

"I guess if I'm going to finish my days playing football, this is the best way to do it," Tanner said as the four us of sat around a table at Sweet Danny's, our favorite barbeque restaurant. The table was loaded up with meat slathered in different sauces, sides of corn bread and beans, and glasses of iced tea. I may have missed a lot of things from Oregon, but the one thing Texas did better than anyone was barbeque.

"You could play in college," Stephen said, but this time his words weren't the start of another fight. Instead, he said it playfully, as a joke. At some point, after a lot of late-night conversations between Tanner, Mom, and Stephen, conversations I wasn't invited to, Tanner said our parents had accepted his decision not to play football. And not just accepted it, but embraced it. When Tanner officially turned down the scholarship, they stood up against some other parents who couldn't believe Tanner's choice.

Tanner waved his forkful of pulled pork at Stephen. "Nope, nope, and nope, but if you want me to tell them you're interested . . ."

Stephen pretended to flex his muscles. "I'm pretty tough. Do you think I can stop a three-hundred-pound lineman?"

"I'm not so sure about you, but Brooklyn could," Tanner said and leaned in closer to us as if telling some kind of secret. "I heard that she held a plank longer than any of the guys on the middle school team the other day at the conditioning class. She's tougher than me!"

"Yeah, well, it's all in a day's work," I casually said, but it was kind of a big deal. A huge deal. I couldn't help but grin when I remembered the looks on their faces when every single one of those boys fell to the floor and I held my plank.

"But I don't have time to play football, I'm going to be too busy dancing at Texas School of the Arts."

"Are you ready for the Showcase?" Mom asked.

"Totally," I said. "And what better timing? Tanner can win the championship next Friday, I'll perform my Showcase pieces to rave reviews on Saturday, and then we'll have the biggest celebration ever on Sunday. How does that sound?"

"The Showcase is Saturday?" Mom asked.

"Yeah, at two p.m."

Mom shot a glance at Stephen that worried me.

"Is there a problem?" I asked.

"The game is next Saturday," Tanner said.

"But what about Friday-night lights?"

"That's regular season play. The championship is always on a Saturday. It gives the teams time to get to Arlington and practice early on the field, and it's easier for parents and students to be there on a weekend."

Parents to be there, I thought. *Parents like Stephen and Mom.*

I took a moment to try to ground myself before I got too upset. I focused on the second hand of the clock as it moved slowly around and thought about the problem and how there was no possible solution but one. I knew the way this was going to play out. It was what I'd been dreading all along.

So before Mom could say anything, I turned to her. I needed to speak up before she made the choice for me. A choice that might not be in my favor. "And you and Stephen can go cheer Tanner on."

"But the Showcase—" Mom started.

I cut her off. "You don't have to go. You'll be able to see

279

me dance a million more times. But the championship is Tanner's last game ever. You can't miss that. I'll be dancing for years and years and years."

"But I *want* to be there to support you."

"I need you and Stephen at the game so you can come back and tell me everything that happened. And then we'll celebrate both of us," I insisted.

"I don't know," Mom hesitated. "Are you sure you don't want me at the Showcase?"

"Positive," I told her, which was a complete lie.

"If you're really okay with it . . . ," Mom said and I pushed down the disappointment that had crept in. I told myself not to cry. I'd told her she could go, so I had no right to get disappointed. Right?

I turned to Tanner instead. "I'm sorry I'll miss your game," I said, and it was true. I'd wanted to see him play. If you'd told me this was going to happen a few months ago, I wouldn't have cared. In fact, I'd have been glad to have an excuse not to go to the game. But now things were different. I wanted Leighton to win, and I wanted to be there to see it. And support Tanner, especially with how supportive he had been to me.

"It's okay," he said. "It's not your fault. We'll both make the town of Leighton proud that day. No one will ever see it coming."

"Still, I wish I could be there."

"You will be. Just not in person. Make sure you impress the heck out of those talent scouts, so you can get into that school, and we'll call it even."

"That's all I have to do?" I asked, and I knew he meant it as a joke, but right then the idea of dancing at all seemed impossible.

"Yep, that won't be a problem, will it?"

"Not at all," I lied. "But that also means you have to promise me to win the championship and maybe set some records along the way."

"Easy, I can do that in my sleep."

Stephen held up his glass of sweet tea. "I propose a toast. To the most talented kids I've ever met. The world will never be the same after next Saturday!"

I picked up my tea, and Tanner and Stephen followed.

"We've got this," I said, but the enthusiasm in my voice was fake, because just like Mom, Logan was going to want to be at that championship game, which meant that if I was going to be a part of the All-City Showcase, I was going to have to dance my solo.

Chapter 52

The thing about football in this town is that it's always going to rule.

Always.

Which was why Logan had to go to the championship game.

He might not play for the high school team yet, but he was a part of it, especially if he wanted to get one of those spots for postseason training with them. I'd heard him talk about proving his dedication to his coach and making a good impression on Coach Trentanelli enough times to know that he had to be there. But I also remembered Logan's promise to me about dancing in the Showcase. I didn't want Logan to have to make the choice between one or the other. It wasn't fair to put him in that position, not after everything he'd done for me. Football meant so much to him, and he had worked so hard. He needed to be at the championship game, and I had to convince him of that.

I figured it would be easier to talk to him in person, so I had to get Tanner's help. I found him watching TV in the family room.

"What's up, twinkle toes?" Tanner asked, using the same term Randy had used, which I'd hated, but somehow, coming from Tanner I was okay with it. It reminded me of the way siblings would tease each other, and I liked the idea of having a brother like that.

"Is there any way you can give me a ride to Logan's house? I need to talk to him, but I promise it won't take long."

"Sure, happy to help. When do you want to go?"

"Now?" I asked, because this had to be like a Band-Aid. It would be easiest to rip it off right away.

"Now it is," Tanner said, and didn't even seem bothered that I interrupted him to take me somewhere. "Let me grab a sweatshirt and we'll leave."

"Thank you," I said, relieved that he was willing to help so easily.

Tanner was back downstairs in a matter of minutes and we headed out to his truck.

"What's the top secret mission you have me going on?" he asked as we pulled out of the driveway.

"It's nothing. I just need to talk to Logan for a minute. In person. "

I told Tanner how to get to Logan's house, and it wasn't long before we were in his driveway.

"I'll try to be quick, okay?" I said as I jumped out of the truck.

Tanner held up his phone and waved it. "Take your time and don't worry about me. I'll watch stupid videos online. Have fun talking dance strategy."

I nodded and didn't bother to correct him.

I wish we were going to talk dance strategy. It stunk that after all our practice and hard work, we wouldn't perform in front of anyone, but I couldn't take the game away from Logan. He had to be there to show his coach and the rest of the team that he was serious about the team, especially since he was part of the postseason training. If he wasn't there, it would look bad.

But how could I dance alone? I was nervous as is about dancing the solo. Could I really depend on only that to get me noticed by the scouts? I didn't know the answers to those questions, but what I did know was that Logan needed to be at that game, so I had to make it at least sound as if I could dance that solo.

I took a deep breath, squared my shoulders like I do before a grand jeté tournant, and headed toward the front door. I pressed the doorbell, and when Logan opened the door, there was no turning back.

"Brooklyn, what are you doing here?" he asked, confused.

"Can we talk for a minute?" I tried to make my voice sound strong and sure, even though I felt anything but.

"Sure. I have a paper I need to write for school, so you've given me a great excuse to procrastinate a little longer."

"Happy to help," I told him and followed him into a small kitchen that was bright and sunny. There was a bowl full of fruit on the table, and Logan pointed to it.

"Do you want something?" he asked.

I grabbed an orange, simply because it would give me something else to do with my hands while I talked to him.

We sat down together and he turned to me, giving me his full attention.

"So what's up?"

"It's about the championship game," I started.

"Coach can't stop talking about how good the team is. He's pretty sure they're going to win. He's told us a bunch of times how we're the next generation of players and we have a legacy to continue. It's scary to live up to those expectations, but also pretty great. He's talking to us like we're real football players."

"Uh, you *are* a real football player," I told him.

"I know, but he's never made us feel that way before. Like, he thinks we're going to do a good job next year when we get to high school. That's so far from how he viewed us at the start of the season. And we're invited to go to the game, too, if we want to. There'll be a bus for any interested middle school players, and we'll get to sit close to the field during the game. It's going to be incredible, and I have you to thank for it."

"You don't have to thank me," I said. "You're the one who helped me. And speaking of help, that's what I wanted to talk to you about. I don't know if you realized it, but the championship game is on the same day as the All-City Showcase."

"Oh shoot, Brooklyn. I didn't even think about that," Logan said, and the excitement in his eyes disappeared.

"It's okay. You don't need to be there," I said before he said anything else.

"Nope, never," Logan immediately said. "I made a promise to you that I wasn't backing out again, and I'm not breaking that promise. No way, no how."

"But I'm giving you permission to. It's not a problem. I'll can still dance my solo."

"Is that enough? I thought you needed to dance with a partner, too," he said.

"A partner would help, but—"

"Exactly," Logan cut in. "Which is why I'm dancing with you."

I held my finger up to signal to him to stop for a minute. "Dancing just the solo is okay. It works for both of us because you don't miss out on the game and I'm still able to showcase what I can do on my own. It's the perfect solution."

Well, it might sound like the perfect solution, if I weren't still so scared to dance the solo and thought I stood a chance against all the other dancers, who were probably amazing.

"But we worked so hard together on the dance," Logan said. "And we don't have to be at the game. It's not mandatory. I can go to the Showcase."

"We did work hard, but at the end, football is your ballet. It's everything. Even if you don't have to go to the game, you need to be there and make sure that you let Coach Trentanelli and Coach Konarski know that you're serious about the team. And I'll dance my solo. This way, we both get what we want. Maybe we can do our dance in the talent show instead. The boys on the team would love that, right?"

"Okay, let's not push it." Logan laughed.

"We'd probably win," I said as Logan picked up his napkin and tossed it at me.

"I just don't know, Brooklyn," Logan said. "The championship game is optional, but being your partner isn't optional in my eyes. I told you that I wasn't going to back out again."

And that's what made Logan such a great person. Football meant more to him than anything in the world, and yet here he was, trying to argue that he should miss the game to dance with me.

"You're not backing out. I'm telling you, it's okay. I'll dance my solo. Besides, weren't you the one who taught me to respect football? And I know how important this game is and how much work you put into improving yourself as an athlete. You need to be at this game. You earned it."

"It doesn't feel right," Logan said reluctantly.

"Believe me," I told him. "Everything about this choice feels right. Go to the game; I'll stun everyone with my incredible solo."

Logan didn't say anything for a long moment, and I could practically see the wheels turning in his head.

"Really, it's okay," I insisted. "This is what I want to do."

He looked as if he was going to fight with me some more, but finally, he nodded.

"All right," he said. "But if you change your mind—"

"I'm not going to change my mind," I assured him and made my voice sound firm. "You're going to that game, and I'm dancing the solo, and that's the way it's going to be."

Logan gave me a half smile. "I guess that's what we'll do if it's what you really want," he said, even though he still didn't sound sure.

"It is," I said and told myself that I had made the right decision. It had to be the right decision, because there was no reversing it now.

Chapter 53

I spent the night before the All-City Showcase on the website for Juilliard's Summer Dance Intensive. I reread the information about it over and over again. I studied the pictures and searched for hashtags about the program. I told myself this was enough. It was what Dasha and I had dreamed about doing. I would be happy with this, and maybe after high school, I could focus on dance in college. I could try other activities and new clubs in school and find other things I liked. I didn't need to eat, sleep, and breathe ballet for the next four years. I told myself these things over and over again until I began to believe them.

What I didn't do was look at TSOTA's website, because I had made the decision not to dance in the Showcase.

Because here's the thing.

I could say that I was going to dance the solo. I could tell everyone that it was okay. But it wasn't. It wasn't at all. Whenever I thought about doing the dance in front of all those talented dancers, I remembered my recital and how I fell.

It was silly to have even thought that I'd be able to

dance alone onstage again. What was I thinking? It was like the universe was sticking its tongue out at me and telling me I was delusional for believing I could dance again after everything that had happened in Oregon. Jayden's broken leg, my hurt ankle, the championship game on the same day: It all made sense now. They were signs, all telling me I was silly for thinking I could do this.

I held the cursor over the link on my Bookmarks bar that I had saved for TSOTA. I hesitated for only a moment before I deleted it from my Favorite Places. I went through and unfollowed it on all of my social media, erasing any trace of it from my life.

Chapter 54

Nothing stops a Saturday FaceTime session with Dasha, so when I woke up on the morning of the big game to dance with her, I headed to the studio to call. I still hadn't decided whether or not I would tell her about not dancing in the Showcase; either option seemed like the wrong choice.

On one hand, she was my oldest and best friend; she deserved to know, but if I told her, she'd try to talk me out of it. That was the type of person that she was, and it was bad enough to admit to myself that I wasn't going to dance, I didn't want to hear about how disappointed she was too.

"I should say something," I said to myself as I waited for her to pick up the FaceTime call.

Dasha's face appeared, and she smiled and gave me a giant wave. "Today is the day! It's your moment to shine! It's here! It's here!"

She jumped up and down and threw her hands in the air. I wished that I could share the same enthusiasm as she did. As I watched her dance around the camera screen, I noticed something.

"Hey, you're not in your garage. Is that the studio?"

Dasha paused and for a moment looked as if she'd been caught doing something she shouldn't, but then her face changed and she was a grinning ball of energy again. "Oh yeah, about that. I was thinking that you don't have to rehearse today. I mean, we've gone over the dance a million times; maybe you shouldn't dance it until this afternoon. We don't want to jinx anything."

"Okaaaaay," I said slowly. This was weird. Very weird. Dasha always made me rehearse, no matter what I said. I was pretty sure that if I were on the way to the hospital some Saturday morning, she'd be FaceTiming me in the ambulance asking me to do the dance one more time.

"I have a much better idea. We figured that you were probably under a lot of stress with the Showcase and needed to let off some of that steam."

"We?"

"Oh yeah, I hope you don't mind, but I invited some friends to come FaceTime with us." Dasha turned her iPad around, and I realized where she was. She was in my old dance studio in Oregon, and the room was full of my friends I used to dance with.

"Am I imagining things?" I asked, confused, surprised, and over-the-moon excited to see everyone.

"Nope! It's real. What do you think? I thought you could use some moral support."

"This is amazing!" I said and waved at all my friends. They looked the same, as if I hadn't moved away and was dropping in on a class. "How are all of you? I've missed you so much!"

Mallory, one of the girls I was superclose to, came up to the camera. "We're excited for you, Brooklyn. You're going to do awesome today."

"Yeah! We can't wait to hear all about it," another girl named Kylie said.

Right. The Showcase.

My good mood evaporated in a second. Everyone was here because of that and they were being so nice to me, while I was living a lie.

"I figured you'd had enough practice and wouldn't want to go through your solo again this morning," Dasha said. "So we had a different idea!"

Loud dance music began to play in the studio. It was one of our favorite "let loose" songs from our weekly hip-hop class.

"We thought that you could use a dance-it-out session with all of us," Dasha said. "You told me how much it helped when you did it at your new studio, so we thought it would be a great thing to try here."

"Are you serious?" I asked, amazed by how right she actually was.

"Oh, I'm dead serious." She turned to the rest of the girls and nodded. "What do you all say? Ready to dance it out for Brooklyn?"

And just like that, all my friends began to dance as if it didn't matter. As if no one was watching, judging, or cared.

I hesitated for only a moment and then let the silliness take over. I shook my arms and legs all over the place to songs that were all about happiness and fun. I let my hair out of its bun, so it fell all over my shoulders. I jumped around, laughed with them, and didn't care what I looked like. And it was perfect. It was exactly what dance was supposed to be: nothing but pure love.

Chapter 55

I thanked Dasha and the other girls about a million times for our Saturday-morning dancing session. What I didn't do was tell them that I wasn't going to dance in the Showcase. How could I? It seemed impossible to say the words after Dasha had planned something as incredible as that. So instead, I allowed them to believe that I was still going to the Showcase.

I wondered how long Tanner kept his decision not to take the scholarship to himself and if this was what he felt like when he first made the choice to turn it down. Was he nervous to tell people? Was he afraid he was going to let everyone down?

These thoughts stuck with me as I huddled next to Mom, Stephen, and Mia in the high school parking lot. We waited with pretty much the entire town to send off the football team to the championship. People were painted up as if it were a Friday night, cars were decorated in Leighton colors, and a large part of the crowd held signs they'd made. We gathered around the bus the team would ride down. They were going early so they'd have some time to practice on the field.

Mom wrapped her arm around me and pulled me close. "I wish I could be in two places at once, but you'll do amazing in the Showcase."

"I hope so," I said and felt a flash of guilt that she thought I was dancing today. That everyone thought I was dancing. I hadn't even told Mary Rose, so I was still on the program for the Showcase. It had all become such a tangled mess that I had no idea how to unravel it. I wished I didn't have to lie, but I couldn't see any other solution.

Members of the team arrived, and each time they did, the band played a drumroll and everyone burst into applause as they headed toward Coach Trentanelli, who stood on the steps at the entrance of the bus. The rest of the team gathered around him and helped welcome each new player who arrived.

It was a pretty elaborate send-off for a football team, and if anyone else saw this, they might have thought a famous celebrity was arriving with the size of the crowd and the way they were going wild. I guess you could say the team was a bunch of famous celebrities, at least to us. Our boys were going to the state championships, and there was no way the town wasn't going to give them a giant send-off.

Mia came over to me with her camera. She was riding down with the middle school football team and considered herself the official journalist for the event.

"So are you ready for your big break?" I asked her.

"You know it!" She grinned and held up a badge around her neck that said OFFICIAL TEAM VIDEOGRAPHER.

"Whoa, fancy. How'd you get that title?"

"I made it!" she said and gave me a sly look. "I figured people wouldn't question someone wearing a badge like this. Who knows what kind of stories I'll be able to get!"

"Just as long as there aren't secrets about Tanner," I joked.

"Nope, never. I've learned that I need approval before running any stories because the aftermath can be tragic."

"A month without my best friend was pretty traumatic," I agreed. "So did you get any good stuff here?"

"Um, have you seen this crowd?" Mia swept her arm around as if I weren't aware of how packed it was there. "I think I've got enough footage to last until I graduate. Everyone wants to talk to me about the team. I asked them to give me their best cheer, and some of it's pretty funny."

"You haven't asked me to do a cheer," I told her.

"Would you?" Mia asked and eyed me skeptically.

"Okay, maybe not, but I love everything about this. The energy in the air is off the charts. Who would've thought I'd be here cheering on the team?"

"It was only a matter of time until we wore you down and turned you into one of us," Mia said. She gestured around to everyone. "You have to admit that you're going to miss this."

"Actually, I'm not," I told her. "I'm not going to miss it at all."

"Really?" Mia asked, and her smile evaporated.

"Surprise!" I said and forced a grin. If I acted excited, maybe I could convince myself to really be okay with all of this. "I'm not going to miss it, because I'm not leaving."

"You're not what?"

"I'm not leaving Leighton. I'm going to go to high school with you."

"Are you kidding?" Mia threw her arms around me. "I get to keep my best friend?"

I nodded and laughed. I tried to wiggle out of her grasp, but she was doing a good job of trapping me in the world's tightest bear hug.

"But what about Texas School of the Arts?" she asked when she finally let go.

I avoided her gaze to make things easier. "I'm not dancing in the Showcase."

"Wait. What! Why? You've been practicing for months. What about Logan? I thought he was doing a great job."

"He is," I said. "But he doesn't love ballet. He loves football. He lives for it. And I wasn't about to take the championship game away from him. So I told him I'd dance alone to make sure he'd go to the game."

"And you're not dancing by yourself?"

I shook my head. "I'm not. I only said that so he'd go to the game. I didn't want him to have to choose the game or me, so I made it easy for him. And now you're stuck with me for the next four years."

I grinned and figured she'd do the same, but instead, she got a stern look on her face and shook her head back and forth.

"Nope, nope, nope. You can't do this. You're dancing in the Showcase," she said.

"It's okay, I don't want to. These last few months have shown me that Leighton isn't all that bad. All I had to do was give it a chance. I already have some ideas for activities and clubs that I might want to join."

"Brooklyn, you have to do this. It's your dream."

"It *was* my dream, but things changed, and now I guess you all are stuck with me." I tried to make a joke about it, but Mia wasn't buying it. She looked at me as if I was making the biggest mistake of my life.

She held up her phone. "Can I show you something?"

She hit the play button on a video and placed it in my hand. Someone was moving across the screen in leaps and twirls. Someone who looked familiar.

"Is this me?" I asked.

She nodded. "I went to your dance studio when I was trying to get you to talk to me. I'd wanted to apologize, but when I got there, you were going over a dance routine by yourself, and I couldn't help but watch. This is the dance you have to do. Look how incredible you are. You need to show all the scouts that at the Showcase. You can't miss this chance."

The recording was from that afternoon when I'd played the music for my recital piece and I'd danced for myself and no one else. The afternoon when I remembered how magical it truly felt to let the music lead you.

I watched myself on the screen, and it was as if I was looking at someone else. The girl on the screen was good. Really good. And maybe Mia was right. But there was no way I could get in front of people and perform that dance again. It was like asking me to do the impossible.

"I can't dance that for anyone," I said.

"Then dance it for yourself," Mia said, repeating those same words Mary Rose had said.

Before I could respond, a huge cheer went up through the crowd. The drill team broke out into a dance, and the band played Leighton's fight song. Tanner had arrived with Malik. The two waved at everyone, and I hadn't thought it was possible, but it got even louder.

"Tanner is invincible," I said. "Even after he decided

not to play football in college, everyone is still in love with him."

"Because he's chasing after his dream," Mia said.

Mia was right. I thought again about how Tanner wasn't letting anyone stop him from doing what he wanted to, even if it wasn't what everyone else expected of him.

I held my hand out to Mia for her phone. "Let me see that video again."

"I can do better," she said and typed something into her phone. "There you go; I sent it to you."

I pulled my own phone out and clicked on the text. I pressed play and watched myself whirl and spin to the music. There was a calm to my face that I hadn't seen in such a long time. I'd placed so much pressure on myself lately to get into TSOTA that I'd forgotten how to simply dance. I missed that peacefulness.

"Hey, listen. I gotta get going," Mia said, interrupting my thoughts. She began to back away, but I reached out and grabbed her arm.

"Why? Where?" I was confused. Did I do something to upset her?

"Tanner's coming over," she said softly. "He's not going to want anything to do with me. Not after my last video."

"Apologize," I told her. "It's as simple as that."

"I don't know . . . ," Mia began.

"I do. I bet you'll find that he forgives you. People are surprising, you know." I spoke to Mia, but I was focused on Logan, who had arrived with his parents. He headed over to the rest of the middle school team and they were all bumping shoulders and joking with each other. Goofing off the way they always did. "After all, you were the one who told me to give Logan a chance."

Mia gave me a halfhearted smile. "I did, didn't I?"

"Yep," I said and pushed her toward Tanner. "Apologize to him. You'll feel a million times better after, and maybe you can talk him into an interview."

"I'd be happy if he just listened to me for a second."

"Go talk to him," I repeated in a firm voice.

"Okay, here I go." Mia took a deep breath and headed toward him. She said something, he nodded, and the two walked away from the group. I turned to give her some privacy and tried to catch Logan's attention instead. He wore his practice jersey and a pair of jeans. All of the boys had red sweatbands on each of their wrists with LHS stitched on in white. When Logan spotted me, he waved and jogged over.

"Today's the day, huh?" he asked.

"Today is the day," I agreed.

"You sure you don't want me to dance with you? It's not too late to change your mind."

"We've gone over this. I'll be fine. You need to go to the game."

"You promise to tell me how it all goes?" he asked, and I nodded, that tiny ball of guilt growing inside of me.

"I sure will," I said. "And make sure you pay attention to the game today, because that's going to be you out there next year."

"I hope so," Logan said and grinned.

I gestured over to Mia, who was recording Tanner with her phone. "It looks like someone is getting the big scoop from the quarterback today."

"Another Tanner exclusive?" he asked with his eyebrow raised.

"Something tells me this one is on slightly better terms."

The two of them talked for a few more minutes and then headed our way. Mom acted as if she hadn't seen Tanner for days, even though she'd seen him at the house only about an hour before. She bounced from foot to foot, talking to him at about a mile a minute. She reminded me of a little kid on Christmas. But this game was a big deal, and it was pretty cool that Tanner was one of the ones leading the way.

Stephen told him how proud he was, and Mom wrapped her arms around him and gave him a giant bear hug. After she let go, he walked over to me and ruffled up my hair. I made a face at him, but it was kind of nice, too, something a brother would do to bug his sister.

"We've got this, right, kiddo?" he asked, and my mood shifted. I hated lying to him. The guilt from my lies sat heavy and deep inside of me, and I felt like a horrible person. "You and I are going to shine, and it's because we're doing what's important to us."

"We are," I told him, my voice low and wobbly. I wanted to say more, but I was afraid if I did, tears would spill out of my eyes. So instead, I nodded and gave him a quick hug.

"You'll wow those judges," he said. "I'm so proud of you."

But I wasn't proud of myself at all. I felt like a traitor as I listened to him. I'd lied to everyone, maybe even myself.

Chapter 56

Tanner and the team left with a send-off fit for kings.

Seriously, the band played the fight song, the cheerleaders led us all in a chant, the drill team did a routine, little kids threw confetti, and the sports boosters shot off fireworks.

Yes, fireworks.

They weren't huge giant ones, but they were loud and spectacular enough to get everyone even more fired up for the game. I was surprised we didn't cause an earthquake with the way we cheered and stomped our feet. I couldn't imagine how loud it would be in the stadium that afternoon and what might happen if they won.

Wait, I take that back: *when* they won. Because I had no doubt that with Tanner leading the team, they were going to bring that title home.

I headed back to the house with Mom and Stephen. The plan was for them to drop me off at home before they began the two-hour trek to the game. I'd told them that Mary Rose was happy to take me so they could go to the game. The lies continued to pile up, and I felt worse and worse inside. Today was supposed to be a happy day full of celebrating and cheering Tanner on, and instead, I was deceiving everyone. When I lied to Logan about doing the solo, I thought I was doing it for a good reason—to convince him to go to the game—but maybe I was wrong. Was there ever a time a lie was good? From the awful way I felt now, I wasn't sure there was.

Stephen drove the car back home, but when he got there, he didn't turn the engine off. Instead, Mom leaned over and gave him a kiss good-bye and jumped out.

"I'll see you later this afternoon," she told him. "Love you."

"Love you back," he said and waved at me. "Good luck, Brooklyn. You'll do great."

"Aren't you going to the game with him?" I asked as Stephen pulled out of the driveway.

"Change of plans. I'm going to drive to the game by myself," Mom said. "I have something more important to do right now."

"More important?" I asked. Leighton was pretty much going to be a ghost town as everyone made the trip to the game. I couldn't imagine what was going on that was more important than getting down there. I was surprised Mom hadn't camped out the night before to get the best seat in the stadium.

"Yep, I have a batch of extraspecial blueberry pancakes to whip up for someone who has a pretty big afternoon. We sent Tanner off to the game with a big to-do; it's only fitting that I do the same for you. What do you think? Do you have time for some pancakes with your mom?"

"Do I? Yes! Yes! Yes!"

I couldn't help it; I threw my arms around her. My response might have been a bit over-the-top, but my goodness, was it amazing to have Mom all to myself.

Mom laughed and gestured toward the house. "All right, then, let's get cooking."

I followed her inside and sat on one of the stools at the island. I cracked the eggs into the bowl for her like I always used to do when we had our surprise pancake breakfasts. Mom turned the radio on, and instead of listening to the local station that blabbed on and on about football, she turned some music on. The two of us sang along as we made breakfast. It was incredible. I had missed this time with Mom, but I hadn't known I missed it this much. Time alone with Mom was everything, and this felt so familiar. If I closed my eyes, I could pretend that the sounds and smells around me were from my old house and we were still in Oregon.

Mom held up a plate full of perfect-looking pancakes and curtsied as if it were the end of a ballet performance.

"Breakfast is served," Mom said.

"I like the sound of that," I told her as I settled into my seat at the table.

I cut a pancake with my fork and put the first bite into my mouth. The blueberries burst open, warm and tart and incredible. I shoveled in a few more bites before I spoke.

"This is so good," I told Mom.

"Isn't it? I don't know why we don't do it more often."

I wanted to tell her that I did. That it was because she was too busy with Stephen and Tanner and her new life. That sometimes it felt as if she had forgotten about me. Instead, I told her how I wished it could be. How I wanted it to be.

"We *could* do this more often," I said.

"We *will* do it more often," Mom agreed, and she said it with such conviction that I couldn't help but believe her. It was the first time in forever that I'd actually felt as if Mom would make time for me, and that made all the difference.

"So tell me," she said. "What are you dancing for your solo? I know nothing about this, which is unbelievable, because I usually know everything about you and ballet."

"You used to," I said softly.

"What?" Mom asked.

I didn't want to ruin this perfect morning, but if I didn't say anything now, when would I? Tanner taught me a thing or two about having the courage to speak up, so if he could do it, I should too.

"You used to know everything about my dancing, but then after you met Stephen, it wasn't important anymore. I felt as if *I* wasn't important anymore." I said the last part quietly, because things like that were hard to speak out loud. They were nearly impossible to say. But it was important stuff, and I needed to get it out. Mom needed to hear it.

"You were never not important. Ever. You're the most important person in my life, and nothing will change that," Mom said so firmly that I almost believed her. But then I remembered how I'd felt when she'd begun to spend more time with Stephen and when she'd missed my recital. She could say one thing, but actions were a lot more important.

"I know you love me," I told her. "But you spend so much time with Stephen and Tanner. You became obsessed with football and are always doing things for the team. It's as if you have forgotten about me."

"Honey, I never meant for you to feel that way. I was trying to make our family work. To show Tanner that he was important to me too."

"But by doing that, it seemed as if I wasn't."

Her eyes got watery, and I thought she was going to cry, which made me feel awful. Mom never cried. She stood up, and before I realized what she was doing, she had scooped me up into the biggest hug in the world. She hugged me so tight that I thought I might pop. She squeezed and she squeezed and instead of fighting it, I let her arms stay around me, where I felt safe and secure and loved.

"You are so important," she said when she finally let go. "And I'm so sorry for making you think for even a second that you weren't. That's never going to happen again."

"Thank you," I whispered. Telling Mom the truth and getting everything out in the open made everything so much better. So much lighter. I didn't realize how much I'd been holding inside. "It's okay."

"It's not," Mom said. "But I'm going to make sure it is."

"That would be nice, because I've really missed you. I've missed us." I gestured to the dirty dishes from the breakfast we had finished. "And I definitely missed all of this."

Mom waved her hands over the dishes as if she were doing a magic spell. "I declare my first step in making sure Brooklyn always knows how truly amazing she is, is to bring back our monthly blueberry pancake breakfasts!"

"Hear, hear!" I yelled and raised a fist in solidarity.

"The second step is to go to the Showcase with you."

"You can't," I said. "It starts at two and the game is at four. There's no way you'd be able to do both."

"Talking to you has made me realize that the only place I want to be is front and center at the Showcase watching you dance."

"But what about Tanner?" I asked.

"I've been to a ton of his games this year. I want to be here for you."

"Mom, it's okay. Go cheer on Tanner. It's his last game, and you should be there," I said, and unlike the other day, when I'd talked Mom out of going to the Showcase because I was afraid she'd make that choice herself, I really did want her to go to the game. Tanner had worked so hard for this, and Mom should be at the game.

"I want to do it," she interrupted. "I'm not doing it to be nice or because I'm your mom. I'm doing it because I love to watch you dance. And this dance is going to be one of your best ever."

"Thanks for the pressure," I joked, but it felt good— really good—to know Mom wanted to be there for me. And a funny thing happened. As the two of us talked, I realized that I did want to dance. Maybe I'd get into the school and maybe I wouldn't, but it wasn't about that any- more. It was about doing what I loved.

"I'd love for you to come and watch me dance again,"

I told her. "But I have to do this myself. I need to prove to myself that I don't have to rely on anyone."

And it was true. There'd be plenty of other shows that she'd be able to come and watch, and after our discussion, I was confident she'd do exactly that. Maybe she hadn't been at my recital, but nothing could change that now. Instead, I needed to have the courage to dance again by myself, so that there would be future shows where she'd be able to come and see me.

"Are you sure?" Mom asked. "I want you to know I'm here for you."

"You are here for me. I understand that now. But today, this is something I have to do myself. And I'm not just saying that to make you feel better. I've got this," I told her, and for the first time in a long time, I really felt like I did. I *could* do this. No, scratch that, I *would* do this.

Chapter 57

Everything between Mom and me felt right again. She gave me another giant hug before leaving for the game, and I had good feelings about us. Really good.

However, as the car drove down the street and out of my sight, I realized one teeny tiny mistake.

I didn't have a ride to the Showcase. I'd forgotten to ask Mom for a ride. I was stuck at home with no way to get there.

I called Mary Rose as soon as I realized my mistake hoping maybe she could drive me, but her phone went straight to voicemail.

I called Mia next, even though I didn't know how she could help.

"I'm going to dance in the Showcase," I said, not even bothering to say hello.

"Duh, that's what I was telling you all along. You can't pass up this chance. Ballet is everything to you."

"You were right, I was wrong," I admitted. "But now there's a serious obstacle in the way."

"What's that?"

"I don't have a way to the Showcase. I mean, I have a bike, but it's kind of far away. And even if I could make it in time, I'd probably be too tired to—"

"Whoa, whoa, whoa," Mia interrupted. "You're not riding your bike."

"You think I should call a taxi? I mean, my parents would kill me, but what other option do I have than my bike? Everyone in this town is at the game."

"I'm not at the game yet."

"I thought you were going down with the middle school team," I told her. "Besides, it's not like you can drive me."

"We're still here. One of the players on the high school team forgot his cleats, so Coach Trentanelli asked that we bring them down. We're about to swing by his house to get them because his mom gave Coach Konarski the garage code."

"Really?" I asked, not sure what was more ridiculous, that someone would forget his cleats on the day of the biggest game of his life or that he'd have to have someone break into his house to get them.

"I couldn't make up a lie as wild as this," Mia said. "Give me five minutes to come up with a plan and I'll call you back."

"You're going to figure this out?" I asked, not believing it for a second.

"Not only am I going to figure it out, I'm going to save the day. What is it they say in ballet, 'It's not over until the fat lady sings'?"

"Um, I think that's for the opera."

"I was close," Mia said. "Just hang in there. I've got this. You'll make it to the Showcase."

And before I could tell her that I wished what she'd said was true, she hung up on me. I paced back and forth in the kitchen, not sure what to do. Could Mia really figure this out? I didn't doubt that she'd try, but I couldn't imagine her actually making it happen.

I grabbed on to the counter as if it were a ballet barre and stretched myself. If there was a chance Mia could get me there, I'd better start warming my muscles now.

I was working on a series of leg extensions when my phone buzzed with a message from Mia.

BE READY IN 10 MIN

READY FOR WHAT? I typed back to her.

10 MIN, she wrote again.

That wasn't like Mia at all. She was all about the full story and making sure you got it—and not just in her reporting, but in her everyday life, too. So this was unusual, but I had to trust her; I had no other options.

I made sure my bag was packed with everything I needed and waited on the front step. My neighborhood was quiet. There were no dogs barking, car horns beeping, or kids yelling to one another. I tried not to watch my watch, but I couldn't help it. Time was passing, and if I didn't get moving, I wasn't going to make it. Was she even the one coming? If so, how? I hoped she had some spectacular plan, but what that was, I had no idea.

I saw a flash of yellow turn onto my street and silently joked with myself that Mia must have sent me a bus. I pictured myself climbing on and riding it all the way to the Showcase. The idea was so absurd that it made me laugh out loud. Well, until the bus stopped in front of my house, the big *whoosh* from the brakes as it settled into a park position pulling me out of my daydream.

The yellow bus was in front of my house.

I repeat, a big yellow school bus was in front of my house.

And Mia hung out the first window.

"Hey, Brooklyn! Yoo-hoo! We're here!" She waved her arms around as if it were impossible to spot this bus in front of my house. As if anyone could ignore it.

And if it wasn't ridiculous enough to see Mia hanging out of the window, the entire middle school team was doing the same.

Every single one of them.

And they all waved and called my name.

"What the heck are you doing?" I asked when she stepped off the bus.

"Taking you to the Showcase." She brandished her arm as if presenting the bus to me. "And not just taking you to the Showcase, but doing it in style."

"Um, it's something, all right. Is this even allowed?"

"Yep. But don't thank me for this awesome idea. Logan is the one who came up with it."

"Logan?" I asked. I had forgotten about him in the midst of all of this. Mia would've had to tell the team the truth, so what must he think? He had to know I'd lied to him, so why would he want to help me?

Mia scurried into the bus and came out with Logan.

"Here, you two talk. I'll save you a seat," she said and left the two of us alone. The other boys pulled up their windows to give us privacy.

The two of us walked over to my front step and took a seat.

"So this was all you?" I asked.

"It was nothing. I told Coach Konarski what was going on and he was happy to help you out. But what I don't get is why you lied to me. Why did you say you were dancing alone before?" he asked.

"I didn't want you to have to make a choice between the Showcase and football. It wasn't fair."

"So you decided for me?" he asked, with a hurt look on his face.

"I thought it was the easiest thing to do," I said.

"I told you that I would've danced with you. I still will. The bus can take both of us to the Showcase," Logan said.

"You don't have to do that for me," I told him.

"Oh, it would be for both of us. We make an amazing team," he said and jumped up and did an exaggerated spin with his hands over his head.

"We do, don't we?" I said and grinned.

"The best," he said. "So, what do you say? Should we go blow those judges away with our amazing lifts and leaps?"

And to emphasize his point, he leapt and twirled around my tree lawn, even as the boys on the team watched from the windows and cheered him on. I couldn't believe this was the same boy who'd ignored me and hadn't wanted to be my partner because he was afraid of what the other boys on the team were going to say. And here he was dancing in front of them all right now without a care in the world.

I wanted to say yes. It would be so much easier than dancing the solo.

But I couldn't.

I had to do this by myself.

If Tanner had taught me anything, it was to believe

in yourself. And that was something that I hadn't done in a long time. Instead, I'd used excuses and let my fear get in the way. Jayden and Logan were crutches for me. If I really wanted to prove to myself that I had what it took for TSOTA, then I needed to dance alone.

"I'd love to dance with you. You've been an amazing partner, and together we probably would rule the dance world, but this is something I need to do alone."

"Are you sure?" he asked. "Because I was looking forward to wearing my polka-dot costume that matches your pajamas."

"Positive. We'll have to save that costume for the talent show," I told him. "You think I'm joking, but we're totally showing the entire school what we've got."

"Only if you promise a rematch for the Mighty Mites game."

I stuck my hand out to him. "You've got yourself a deal."

He took my hand, and the two of us shook.

It's almost impossible to think about how much I wanted to get out of this place when I first moved here. Now I could say that I was happy. Very happy. In fact, one might even say I was starting to feel like a true Texan. And who knew that two of my biggest fans would end up being football players?

A loud horn startled Logan and me out of our little heart-to-heart moment.

"Let's get a move on!" Mia yelled out the window. "We've got the Showcase to get to."

The two of us climbed onto the bus, and the driver pulled out of my development as fast as she could without speeding.

"You really outdid yourself today," I told Mia.

"That's what friends do," Mia said. "They bring entire school buses when you need help."

"If that's not a good friend, I don't know what is," I told her.

Everyone talked and joked on the way to TSOTA, and we made it there with twenty minutes to spare.

"You've got this," Mia whispered to me and gave me a giant hug. "In fact, I'm going to be really mad if I see you around Leighton High next year."

"Oh, now you want to get rid of me?"

"Yep, if someone has as much talent as you, the only place you belong is TSOTA. But don't forget that we have a standing date for burritos once a week and Friday-night lights."

"I'm never going to get away from football, am I?"

"You couldn't even if you tried," Mia said, and something told me she was right.

But as I got off that bus and the middle school football team, the same boys who I had hated at the start of the school year for invading my dance studio, hung out of the windows and cheered and wished me luck, I was pretty sure I'd be okay with that. Because home wasn't always a place or a location. Home was where you felt like you belonged, and even if I fought the football fever, I had to admit that Leighton was a part of me. And I was a part of Leighton.

Chapter 58

I waved one last time at everyone on the bus and headed into the theater where the Showcase was being held. I have to admit that after the send-off the middle school football team had given me, I was feeling pretty good.

You've got this, Brooklyn, I told myself. *You're going to dance better than you've ever danced before, and everyone in the audience will be wowed beyond belief!*

It's amazing what a bus full of your fans can do. I practically strutted up the front steps and right into the lobby.

A lobby full of dancers.

There were so many dancers.

And they all looked completely relaxed. The opposite of how I felt at the moment. Some stretched, while others talked and joked with each other, texted on their phones, or listened to music on headphones. I doubted any of them had stomachs that were turning somersaults like mine was.

And just like that, my confidence quickly vanished as I took everyone in.

There are only six spots open, a voice inside my head said, and the doubt crept in. *Remember the last time you danced alone? Do you really think you can get up onstage and compete against these people? What if you forget your steps? What if you fall?*

"What was I thinking?" I asked out loud. A wave of panic settled over me so it was as if I were drowning. A million billion thoughts raced through my mind, and not one of them was good.

"This was a bad idea," I told myself. "A very bad idea."

I needed to get out of there. I wasn't ready for this. It had been silly to think I could dance a solo again. I was headed toward the doors when I heard my name being called.

"Brooklyn! Over here!"

I spotted a group in the corner waving their hands around to get my attention. I did a double take, because there, yelling my name, were Elliana, Adeline, and Jayden. I made my way through the crowd to them. I didn't think I'd ever been more relieved to see some familiar faces.

"What are you all doing here?" I asked.

"We're your biggest fan club," Jayden said.

"And my only," I told him. "Seriously, what's going on? I figured you'd be with your family, cheering on your brother and the rest of the team."

"Silly girl," Jayden said. "You're the star. We wanted to be here for you."

"You didn't think we'd leave you all alone to perform, did you?" Adeline asked. "The whole town might be cheering on the football team today, but they're the ones who are wrong. The All-City Showcase is the place to be."

I gestured around to the room packed full of other dance hopefuls. "Obviously. Look how many people are here."

"You're going to do an amazing job," Elliana said and gave me a hug. "I can't believe that I'm going to be able to say that I have a friend who goes to TSOTA."

"Whoa, let's hold up a bit," I said holding up my hand in the stop position. "Let's not get ahead of ourselves. I need to get through the dance first, and right now I'm not feeling it at all. I'm scared out of my mind."

"Then you're perfectly normal, "Jayden said. "If you weren't scared, I'd think something was wrong with you. We all get stage fright before a big performance."

"Yeah, and I usually throw up before I have to dance in front of an audience," Adeline said, and when she saw our grossed-out faces, she shrugged. "What? It happens. And once I do, I'm ready to take on the world."

"I don't know," I said. "I had a really bad experience the last time I danced in front of a big audience. And the pressure might be too much. Look at all these other dancers. How in the world can I compete with everyone?"

"Then don't," Elliana said.

"Don't what?"

"Don't worry about the other dancers and the judges. Just dance because you love it."

"Just dance," I repeated, which seemed to be the mantra from pretty much everyone around me.

Jayden gave me a push toward the registration table. "Go check in and warm up. Don't doubt yourself for a second. You've got this."

"You really think I can do this?" I asked them.

"We know you can," Adeline said, and Jayden and Elliana nodded in agreement. "Now get over here and let's have a group hug."

And that's exactly what we did. I stepped into my friends' arms and let them envelop me. And maybe we looked silly standing in the middle of the room hugging like that, but in that moment, I felt so loved and supported, I couldn't help but strut over to that registration table.

"I'm Brooklyn Gartner," I told the woman and paused. I glanced over to my friends, who waved wildly and gave me thumbs-up signs. I laughed softly to myself before turning back to the woman. "And I'm ready to dance."

And it was true.

I was ready.

I was so ready.

Chapter 59

Dancing in the All-City Showcase was a lot different from my recital, and I think that helped. Instead of wearing the white nightgown that Clara has in the show, I wore my leotard and tights. And the stage was empty, with no sets or props. It made it easier to pretend that this was a rehearsal. That I was in the studio or my basement and not about to perform the biggest dance of my life.

I stepped out onto the stage and stood in the center, where a spotlight was focused. The stage lights above glowed so bright that the audience was nothing but a blank black space.

All this time I had been worried about whether or not Mom was in the audience, but it wouldn't have even mattered. I couldn't see anyone sitting out there.

And I realized was that they didn't need to be sitting out there for me to feel their love and support. It covered me like the old quilt my grandma had made, familiar and warm.

I thought about how lucky I was in that moment. About everyone who had brought me to that point and what I carried from each of them. They might not have all been there physically, but that didn't mean that they weren't with me. As I stood on that stage, I knew every one of them was cheering me on.

I closed my eyes and pictured them all.

An amazing mom who had believed in me from the start.

A stepbrother who taught me how important it was to chase my dreams.

A stepdad who encouraged me as much as he did his own son.

A best friend from Oregon who never let me give up.

A best friend from Texas who reminded me what it meant to dance.

A bus full of middle school football players who understood hard work and what it can do for you.

A dance partner who taught me to see this town in a different way.

A dance teacher who trusted in my talent.

And the best classmates ever, who had shown up to remind me that I could do this.

I carried every single one of them with me.

I'd been so afraid to go up and dance onstage alone, but the thing was, I'd never been alone.

The speakers crackled and a woman's voice announced me.

"Dancer twenty-three is Brooklyn Gartner. She is in

eighth grade and dances at Center Stage Dance Studio."

"This is it," I whispered to myself. "You can do it."

I stepped into third position and waited for my turn to show them all what I could do.

The music started, and I counted the first measures. It filled my veins, coursing through me until it invaded every part of me and I couldn't think of anything but the music and the movement and that moment.

I shut out the world around me.

I let go of the past.

I ignored my fears, and the audience disappeared.

I was muscle and strength and beauty.

The world was gone, and it was me and my love for ballet—and it was incredible.

I'd been so wrong about dancing onstage again. I had thought I didn't belong here, but it was the exact opposite. As I moved through the steps, I realized that this was where I was supposed to be. This was what I had been searching for. This was what I had needed to find again.

Because there, on that stage, I was home.

Chapter 60

After I finished dancing, I went back into the theater and grabbed a seat in the back, where I watched the rest of the dancers. There were some really skilled people onstage, and it was incredible to think Mary Rose had thought I was good enough to be in the Showcase with them.

After the last dancer performed and the lights in the theater came on, everyone poured out. I scanned the crowd for my friends, but it wasn't their faces that I saw coming up the aisle.

"Mom?" I asked, totally confused.

"Honey," she said with a huge smile on her face. "You were amazing."

I moved into the aisle so she could come in and avoid the crowd heading out. She handed me a giant bouquet of flowers, which I accepted, still in disbelief.

"What are you doing here?" I asked.

"Don't be mad at me," she started. "I know you wanted to do this yourself, but I couldn't miss your performance. There's nothing that I love more in the world than seeing you dance. And for what it's worth, you didn't know I was here; you did it thinking I wasn't."

"But what about the game?"

"Stephen is there to support Tanner, and Mia promised to record everything for me so that the two of us can watch it together. This is where I needed to be. There was never any question about that."

"I'm glad you came," I told her and wrapped my arms around her in a hug. I thought about how true my words were, because having Mom here made everything a million times better.

"I am too," she whispered into my ear, and I couldn't believe how lucky I was to have a mom as incredible as mine.

The two of us pulled apart as a woman came up the aisle toward me.

"Brooklyn Gartner?" she asked, and when I nodded, she extended her hand to both Mom and me. "I'm Eliza Carter. I'm one of the teachers at Texas School of the Arts. I was happy to see that you checked our school on the Showcase form for programs that you're interested in. You'll get an official invitation in the mail in about a week, but I wanted to let you know that we'd love for you to audition for the school."

"You would?" I asked, and I was pretty sure my jaw dropped all the way to the floor.

She laughed politely and nodded. "Your dancing was very impressive, and we're excited to learn more about you."

"Thank you, thank you very much," I said and tried to play it cool, but was that even possible during a moment like this? She walked out of the theater, and I turned to Mom. "Oh my gosh, oh my gosh, oh my gosh! Did that just happen?"

"It did, and you deserve it," Mom said, and the two of us jumped up and down in excitement, because what else were you supposed to do when you found out that TSOTA was interested in you?

"This is the best news in the world," Mom said, and I couldn't have agreed more.

Chapter 61

The next evening we sat around the kitchen table celebrating, because the football team did something incredible: They brought home the state championship, and Tanner had an amazing game. The town couldn't have been more excited. And I was a very proud sister.

"Are you sure you don't want to celebrate with the team?" Stephen asked as Tanner dished up another heaping helping of Mom's lasagna. We were all seated around the dinner table, eating our food a little too fast because Mom had bought a German chocolate cake to eat for dessert.

"Nope, this is where I want to be," Tanner said. "I can meet up with some of those guys after dinner. But for now, I want to spend time with all of you. With my family."

Mom beamed, and I was pretty sure she swept a tear away from her eye.

"Speaking of being where I want to be, I was looking at housing at UT, and it seems a lot easier to stay here for the first year or two. I could save a ton of money if I did that. What do you think?"

Mom's face lit up. "That would be wonderful. We'd love to have you around here longer."

Stephen nodded in agreement. "You're always welcome here."

Tanner turned toward me. "What about you, Brooklyn? Could you handle having your stepbrother around a little bit longer?"

"Brother," I said to Tanner. "Forget the 'step' part. You're my brother, and I think it would be great to have you around."

Tanner grinned, and I thought about what I'd just said. About Tanner and family and being there for everyone. You don't get to pick who your family is, but you're pretty lucky when your family ends up being people you would want to pick. And this family would always be my first choice. Always.

ACKNOWLEDGMENTS

Much like football, writing is a team effort, and I've been so lucky for the group of people that surrounded and supported me as I wrote this book.

As always, thank you to my incredible agent, Natalie Lakosil, who has always been one of my book's biggest cheerleaders.

I'm so lucky to have been able to work on my fourth book with my amazing editor, Alyson Heller. I couldn't ask for a better editor and your ideas, insights, and suggestions always make the book sparkle and shine. A thank you also to the dream team at Simon & Schuster, Elizabeth Mims, Sara Berko, and Jessica Handelman, who never fail to help create a finished product that I love.

There is nothing greater than being able to write for the audience that I teach. Thank you to the Perry Local School District for your never-ending support, and a special shout out to the Writer's Club, High School English Department, and librarian-extradionaire, Jodi Rzeszotarski.

Thank you to Chris Bezzeg, who answered all the random questions I texted him about football. Your expertise is much appreciated, and any mistakes in the book with descriptions of football are all my own.

I started taking dance classes when I was young, and while it wasn't smooth sailing from the beginning (I was a fan of freezing up and not moving while everyone danced around me!), I have such amazing memories of my time spent in studios with some of the best teachers and friends. A special thanks to my first teacher, Jeanne Hollick, who had to put up with my personal "invented" choreography, and dance partner and BFF, Betsy Kahl. Whether the two of us were dancing together in class, on stage, or in my bedroom to Michael Jackson or Madonna, nothing beat our moves, and your white stag role will go down in history for its epicness.

A million thanks to my readers; I write these books for you! There is nothing better than hearing from those of you who have reached out and sent letters and e-mails. I love you all and it's so incredible to be able to write the stories I would have wanted to read when I was your age.

Thank you to my WSS, Elle La Marca for all the motivation, chat sessions, and plot whispering, and for just being your awesome self!

My family has always been my first cheerleaders and I could never thank you enough for your endless support, enthusiasm, and kind words.

Brooklyn, Addie, Ellie, Calvin, and Maggie . . . thank

you for being the greatest nieces and nephew in the world! I've loved being a part of your lives and watching you grow as you become amazing individuals with such fun, smart, and silly personalities. Spending time with all of you is one of my favorite things to do!

And to Nolan, my little writing buddy from the day you were born. You inspire me to be better and to do better for the world. Your personality, creativity, and imagination remind me so much of myself when I was young and every day is a new amazing adventure with you. I'm in awe at the person you are becoming and am so honored to be your mom.

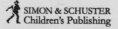